DIAMONDS & DEMONS

BEAUTIFUL BEASTS ACADEMY

KIM FAULKS

MILA YOUNG

Thank you to the most phenomenal readers out there, to our hard working Alpha readers and Betas, your enthusiasm and excitement is infectious. Thank you to J.C. Hart, our phenomenal editor, and Tory our brilliant proofreader. We couldn't pull this off without you.

Mila: A huge thanks and appreciation to my hubby for his constant support and love through everything. Even when he calls Kim my wife haha. Love you babe.

Kim: To my husband, for understanding when I'm always in the study with the door closed, I love you with all my heart.

Join our Kila Foung reader group by clicking on the image below and joining the shenanigans!

LIONS AND LIES
MILA YOUNG
KIM FAULKS

A best friend is more than someone who shares laughter and tears...
They also know the best places to hide a body.

Academy life isn't what I expected. Fangs, fur...demonic bunnies everywhere we turn.
Oh, and the Wolves.
Three gorgeous Wolves who make my dead heart come to life.
Judas, Bond...and Nero.
Add in a sexy new Vamp teacher and my new role as Understudy to the most Ancient and powerful of our kind, and you've got one hot and conflicted class schedule.

But as classes begin, yet another creature stumbles into my room in the dead of night.
And he leaves behind a bag filled with diamonds.
Only they're not like any diamonds I've ever seen before.
Darkness moves through the halls at Bestias Academy. A new threat makes itself known.

And it's got its sight set on me.

My world becomes three things.
Diamonds, Demons and death....

Note: No Demon bunnies were harmed in the making of this story. Slow burn Reverse Harem with kickass characters and hunky wolves.

CHAPTER ONE

PREDATOR BECOMES THE PREY

"Get yourself ready." Ms. Amoret Lucas clasped her hands together, her eyes glinting as she scanned the room, stilling on Ava sitting beside me. "We're going to be having *another* mock hunt this morning."

The entire class groaned in unison.

Bitching and snarling rippled through every student.

But not me.

And not the rest of my crew.

Another mock hunt? Even after we'd gone to Principal Stone and begged her no more killing of animals. She didn't care about what we wanted. She'd never even lifted her gaze from the paperwork on her desk.

Instead she just muttered, "*I'll look into it,*" and shoed us away with the wave of her hand.

That had been three days ago.

Plenty of time to make sure the mock hunt didn't go ahead.

I turned my head, catching Ava cross her arms against her PETA t-shirt, which exclaimed, *Animals have rights!* She'd taken a stance against these mock hunts that used real live bait, and so help us to the Ancients and back...we were gonna back her. She'd tied her blonde hair into a ponytail and painted dark make-up around her eyes, reminding me of a warrior. Guess that was the look she was going for.

Ms. Lucas cut a glare across the mass of bodies in the class and snapped. *"That's enough."* There was a second where the manic gleam in her eyes shone a little brighter. *"This class* will not be dictated to. We will not be bullied. We will *not* bow down to the *whims* of the select few."

"Whims?" Ava snarled. *"Whims?"*

I reached out, placed one hand against her arm, stilling her rage. Ms. Lucas had turned into a right royal bitch in the interim from last semester. But it didn't matter...she wasn't the only one who'd changed.

I glanced at the schedule, freezing at the lone class standing out above all the rest. It was a class for one...a class designed for the Understudy of the Ancient.

A class especially for me.

I shuddered, swallowing my excitement. Once the mayhem following my birthday party had died down and Hermond had been dealt with by the Ancient, I'd attended the Great Hall and met with the Ancient Vampire in private.

I glanced at Ava, who turned and met my gaze with a savage smirk as I struggled to find an adequate description for the meeting. It had been...*unusual,* to say the least.

Chairs scraped against the floor. I turned to the three Wolves, who hadn't moved, and one by one they turned to meet me. *Judas,* the dark brown-eyed Alpha who just exuded sex appeal, and Bond, the sandy-haired Beta behind him, were all business, making an imposing duo, but add in Nero, the raven haired, blue-eyed Wolf and you had a pack that ruled the hallways of this Academy.

Each one turned their gaze to find mine, and I was lost within the power, drunk on desire...overcome with *L...that word*. The word I wasn't saying. No way, no how. And I suddenly forgot to how to move, remembering Nero saying their pack shares. Did that mean sharing a girlfriend? Hell, were we official now? But how would it work?

Especially with my father hating their kind....

With everything I'd seen and experienced lately, it felt like the entire world seemed to be hovering on a knife's edge; tensions were high. All we needed was one goddamn *push* and chaos would descend and the Beasts would go to war with one another...and the only ones who'd come out winners were the Witches waiting in the wings, ready to come in and steal all the money and the power they could get their greedy little hands on.

"Let's go...*now!*" Ms. Lucas snarled from the doorway as the rest of the class filed out like good little students.

I shoved my chair backwards, Ava and the boys followed. A bitter breeze carved through the hallway to burst through the open door, making me reach for my jacket. But the icy gust wasn't the only thing making me and the others pile thick, down jackets over our immortal bodies.

Empty glass vials clinked in the pockets. A smile curled my lips as I shrugged the jacket on and headed for the doorway, listening to the heavy footfalls behind me.

"Looks like it's going to be a killer day out there, Ms. Lucas," Ava muttered as she passed.

I stifled a snigger and followed the rest of the class along the hallway and then out of the main building of Bestias Academy.

The name was fitting. We were *beasts* in more ways than one. Vampires, Shifters, Ghouls, and Demons. We all congregated within these walls, studying to be better.

Just not today.

Today we were saviors, even if we'd infected the most helpless rabbits with Demon blood. We had a lesson to teach the teachers.

Cat-calls and hoots of laughter followed the sniggers and growls. Even though they hated the inconvenience of another hunt, they were more than ready for an excuse to rip and tear. Ms. Lucas was perfectly fine adding more bunnies to the long list of *training equipment* we used.

"I've got a surprise this time!" she called out as we stepped into the wooded area of the ground of our school. "I managed to find ten rabbits. I've not numbered them this time. I want you to grab as many as you can."

"Yeah! Looks like rabbit for breakfast!" one of the guys roared.

"Ms. Lucas," Ava spoke loud enough to draw her gaze. "I'm going to ask you one more time. Please reconsider this, it's a cruel and unnecessary act."

But the Demon shone on the teacher's gaze, hazel eyes changed to black for a heartbeat before they were murky green once more. "This is going ahead," she snarled with a curl of her lips. "Whether you like it or not."

I shoved my hands into my pockets, one curling around the three empty vials, and the other a set of clamps...that were supposed to be around the locks on the rabbits' cages.

"Okay," Ava said slowly and calmly...a little *too* calmly as she glanced to me. "We tried."

"We sure did," I murmured and followed the rest of the class.

One glance at the Wolves and they just gave a shrug, ready to carry out our plan.

Ms. Lucas, sick of waiting, surged forward with the rest

of the class. There was almost a goddamn hitch in her step in her excitement.

Nesrin and her cat gang turned and stared at us. They were wary after what happened at my birthday party. There hadn't been one snarl, or hiss from any of them since.

They were waiting for someone to push us, before we pushed back. Then they'd know exactly how strong our little band of misfits was. The events of my birthday party had solidified an unspoken pact between Ava, me and the Wolves. The guys had jumped in and helped without question. They'd put their lives in danger, and in my books, that made them friends. Well, more... but I wasn't ready to decipher those emotions yet.

"Are you ready, class?" Ms. Lucas called out.

I dragged my hand from my pocket, clutching the empty vials. Remnants of black demon blood clung to the sides and pooled at the bottom. Blood that was now racing through the bunnies like lightning. Nesrin's eyes widened, as the clasps jingled in my other hand and Ms. Lucas' frantic words tore through the trees in the distance.

"Oh my...*wait...WAIT! Run!*" she screamed and screamed and screamed.

The terrified sounds of predators turned prey almost warmed my undead heart from the bitter grasp of the winter wind.

"You'd better run," I murmured to Nesrin and the others. Brylee wrenched her gaze to movement as a tiny gray rabbit tore from the clearing, the perfect, soft downy, white fur of its nose already soaked with crimson blood. It hissed.

Terrified wails filled the air as the five of us turned and ran.

And the screams carried all the way through the open

doors of the main building as we passed through and along the halls. Teachers and students stopped and stared. Principal Stone stepped out of her office, her gaze drifting to the tortuous sound.

School was back bitches.

And this time we weren't going to be pushed around.

CHAPTER TWO

WHAT THE HELL KIND OF NAME IS NEFARIOUS ANYWAY?

WE SAT IN OUR SEATS IN THE CLASSROOM, WAITING TO see who would be the first of the other students to step in. Nesrin, the Panther shifter. I'd figured Brylee, knowing a Cheetah was more cunning when it came to survival.

I guess I was wrong.

Salome followed them into the room, golden Lion eyes flashing with the hunter that lay within as she took her seat behind her Alpha...and Brylee was last, the Cheetah shifter slinking in. They slipped quietly into their seats as outside, three of our class tore from the tree line wailing and flapping their arms like madmen.

The sight was hilarious.

Still, none of us laughed, only sat in chilling silence...and finally Ms. Lucas stumbled through the open door. Her hair was a bird's nest on top of her head. Deep, bloody gouges had been carved across her cheek. Her glasses were broken in the middle, the two lenses wobbling on top of her cheekbones.

"Ms. Lucas." Principal Stone raised her voice, warily

following her through the open classroom door. "Is everything okay?"

But the teacher didn't answer, only pulled out her chair and sat carefully down. The front of her brown knitted cardigan was a mess of frayed woolen strands. Cuts and blood covered both hands as she reached for a drawer at the bottom of her desk and lifted out a bottle of gin. I should have felt guilty for hurting her, but maybe this would make her see that using live bait wasn't the best way to teach her hunting class.

"Ms. Lucas," Principal Stone murmured and cut a careful gaze toward the rest of us.

Still we said nothing, only listened as our teacher murmured. "I'll b-be m-aking some adjustments to the sc-schedule...n-n-no m-mm...mmm...more mock hunts."

A smile curled the corners of my mouth.

One brow rose on the Principal's face before it lowered once more and she turned that critical stare toward us. "I suppose this is *your* doing?"

"Not us, Principal," Judas answered sweetly. "We're just holding a silent, *amicable* protest on the rabbits' behalf."

"Mmmhmmm." She pursed her lips and then stepped toward the teacher. "It's okay Amoret, drink your gin. I'm sure future mock hunts will go well." Ms. Stone turned, hard eyes finding each one of us. "We will find out who tainted the rabbits, and there will be repercussions."

"Bring it on," I muttered. "I'll take whatever detention you're ready to dish out."

Small wordless murmurs spilled past the teacher's lips as she lifted the glass and drank. I stared at the clock, watching the hands tick as the next lesson drew close.

"I don't like this." Ava turned to me. "I don't like you going to that special class without me."

"It's not special." That word made me sound *special*. "It's just *specialized*."

Ms. Lucas remained slouched in her chair, almost dazed, a droplet of blood dripping down her cheek, its metallic tang teasing my nostrils. Fresh. Warm. But I wasn't hungry...only amused as the rest of the class slowly crawled in, bloody, frazzled, eyes wide in horror. One of them even had a tuft of brown fur on the end of his nose. A bark of laughter tore from Judas, before he bit the sides of his mouth and lowered his gaze.

The rest of the lesson passed in stunned silence, with frantic gazes whenever a squeal tore through the air, until finally the bell trilled, and everyone jumped to their feet, grabbing their books, and scrambling out of class.

Ava just looked sad and lonely. She waved at me before heading in the opposite direction.

"So, what are you doing tonight?" Bond asked, nudging my arm gently with his shoulder, while Judas walked on my other side. Nero walked backward in front of us, not looking where he was going. *Cocky much?*

"Studying for our quiz," I answered, knowing full well where this was going. "Why?"

"Cafeteria is serving milkshakes and brownies tonight," Judas added.

"And we heard they'll have a blood variation." Nero rubbed his tummy in exaggeration circles. "Yum."

"Are you asking me out on a date?"

"Depends, is Ava coming?" Bond murmured seductively.

I shook my head and chuckled. "There's no way she's missing out on milkshakes."

He nodded, and gave a shrug. "Then it's not a date."

Were they really hinting at a date...with all three of them at once? So that whole thing about a pack sharing *was* real. Questions. I was full of them. I lifted my gaze to a wooden door marked *L - Ancient Arts.* "This is my stop."

Nero peered through the window in the door. "Looks like no one's here. You want us to keep you company?" He turned back with a cocky smile.

"No." I laughed. "It's part of being the Ancient's Understudy. Lucky me, hey."

"Yeah, it's gonna suck, your teacher is vile," Nero continued.

I stiffened. "Vile?"

"Yeah." He took my hand, drawing me away from the door as the other two Wolves peered into the room. "Miss the class. He won't even notice you're gone."

"What are you talking about?" I glanced over my shoulder. Bond and Judas stepped away as the door opened from inside.

Pale skin. Striking pale blue eyes. It was all I saw...and then the tatts...*all of them,* running down the length if his arms. He was the kind of Vampire who'd stop me in my tracks. Perfect bone structure, thick brows crowning piercing eyes, and red parted lips complete with tousled midnight hair. The only thing missing was fangs.

"See," Nero whispered. "Vile."

"Miss Livingstone, this way," the gorgeous hunk murmured. It was like sex had just strolled into my life...*no, no it sauntered, swaggered even.* I couldn't think...couldn't even form a complete sentence.

I swallowed hard.

He opened the door wider. A low snarl slipped into the air. I jerked my gaze toward the sound, catching Judas and the others staring at me. I swallowed hard. "Sure, yep. Coming Sir."

"Better not be," I caught the snarl from Judas before he took one last look at my new teacher and then backed away.

The others followed, giving the teacher one last glare before leaving.

"Welcome to your Ancient Arts class. I'm Professor Leathers."

Come again? I jerked my head toward him as he turned. I stifled a snigger.

"Something funny?"

"*No,*" The word tore from my lips. "People just call me Mor, Professor...*Professor L...* Maybe we use each other's first names?"

He leaned against the table at the front of the room, biceps bulged as he folded his arms. "Good idea. Call me, Nefarious."

"Are you kidding? Nefarious Leathers?"

He just chuckled and shook his head. "Ridiculous, huh? My parents had a wicked sense of humor. I see you've drawn the attention of the Wolves."

Blue eyes sparkled as he studied me, and Dad's voice was all I heard. *Wolves and Vampires don't mix.*

"Is that going to be a problem?"

I waited for anger and the disappointment. God knows I'd had enough from Dad over the past few weeks during semester break. I didn't need anyone else breaking my balls.

"Not at all," he answered and uncrossed his arms. "I believe Supernaturals *should* work together. Vampires and Wolves. Beasts and Witches. There are two sides to every coin, Mor. The question becomes not what *you* want, but what is best for the greater community."

I slipped into a seat in front of him. It seemed weird

being the only student here, but this didn't feel like any class I'd had before. This felt like a discussion....

I pressed my spine against my seat. "What if the community doesn't know what's good for them?"

He broke into a loud laughter, the sound rippling like thunder. "As Plato said, no one is more hated than he who speaks the truth. People don't want to be told they're wrong. *But* you're thinking in the right direction, and questioning things, which I like. You're going to need that. Before we get too philosophical, you recently met with Vlad Vasile, our Ancient, right?"

"Yes," I muttered and glanced at the table. *Shit...shit..shit.* Maybe he won't ask me what he was really like...maybe I can just be *diplomatic* and not say a damn thing at all. I just smiled and nodded.

"You know, I attended the Great Hall a number of times, interviewed him for my thesis. He is quite a...*character.*"

I flinched and jerked my gaze to his.

"Tell me." He leaned forward, "Is the old fart still cross dressing?"

A cough tore free, burning and savage through my chest. I lunged forward, grasped the corner of the desk and hacked and wheezed.

"Hey." He slammed a palm against my back. "You okay?"

I nodded even though the room was blurring under a sheen of tears until I could finally breathe, and then I wiped the tears from my eyes.

"What do you think your role as his Understudy is?" Mr. Leathers strode back to the front of the class and turned, gripping the table on either side of him.

I chewed on my cheek, swallowed the burn and tried to

speak. "Help the Ancients rule over the clans, amongst other...*things.*"

Mr. Leathers' eyes narrowed, and clearly, I'd said the wrong thing.

Air rushed from his lips with a sigh as he gripped his hips. "Other things, huh? *Okay,* what did he do?"

"What?" I leaned forward convinced I heard him say to me, "what did he make you do?"

"Come on, what did Vlad say to you?"

Oh God. I stared up at the ceiling, wishing I could forget this. But still the primal throaty purr rolled through my head. "He said the best thing about being a Vampire is being sexy."

The teacher stared at me, then cleared his throat. "Sexy, huh?"

There was stunned silence, before his eyes twinkled and his lips curled. A roar of laughter tore from his lips as Nefarious shook his head and then cocked it, staring at me. "Did he really?"

I nodded, smiling and shaking my head. "I couldn't believe it myself. I mean...he's like what? *Two thousand years old?*"

"At least." He chuckled and threw one leg casually over the corner of the desk. "He's unusual to say the least. You know when I was there, he made me sit on the end of his bed while he cat-walked his entire collection of dresses for me."

"*No...*" I muttered, shock stilling me cold.

"Oh yes. There's never a dull moment at the Great Hall believe me. It makes you think about the switch from his more, public life. There's a certain sacrifice to being his understudy, it's just part of the job."

"Sacrifice?"

The laughter seemed to slip away from his eyes. "Your friends for example. There's a lot of study, a lot of *pretense* you have to uphold. You might find it difficult to juggle social events."

"Why? Why can't I just be normal? Why does this have to change who I am?"

"Because," Mr. Leathers leaned closer. "You aren't like *them*. You are hand-picked by the Ancient himself and you'll be privy to a lot of guarded secrets of our kind. This kind of status comes with sacrifices, and the communication with your friends is one of them."

I glanced toward the doorway.

"Anyway, enough of that." Mr. Leathers smiled again. "You don't need to worry about that now. Let's begin with the responsibilities of an Ancient." He counted on his fingers. "Unite Vampire Clans. Be the ambassador between humans and Vampires and Shifters. Claim territory for the clans under his command. Keep peace with other Ancients. Mediator for any mortal media, and ensure constant supply of blood to the clans."

My head spun trying to remember everything. I reached into my bag, yanked out a notepad and started to scribble. It made sense, but my mind circled his last point. "How does he ensure a supply of blood?"

"Agreements with donor groups. We don't share them with other jurisdictions, and it's a touchy topic." After leaning over and pulling a leather-bound book out of his bag, he came over, and placed it on the edge of my table.

I dusted the cover of dust, and when I opened it, the spine creaked. Inside, each page looked to be handwritten. "How old is this thing? It must weight a ton. Isn't there a version on USB I can use?"

"These are ancient texts and unfortunately we don't have it on a memory stick. But we'll take it slow...*for now.*"

I stared at the Latin wording and ancient text and sighed. All this in one class?

Being a damn Understudy might be the end of me yet.

CHAPTER THREE

NEW CLASSES. NEW RULES

Ava snapped her head up and her gaze cut across the cafeteria to meet mine. I knew that look. Knew it meant only one thing...*trouble.* The boys turned their heads as I carried the tome with me. Judas glanced at the book, so did every other person in the dining hall...teachers included.

"Damn," Ava muttered her gaze drifting to the book. "You're gonna be buff as Hell hauling that thing around."

I dropped it on the table with a deafening *thud* and winced. "Tell me about it."

The Wolves strode toward us and then slid along the bench seat, first Judas, then Bond and Nero.

"What was the class like? Who is your teacher? What was your first lesson? What kind of things will you be studying? Do you have excursions? Can you bring a friend?" Ava's lips barely moved and yet she fired off questions like a semi-automatic gun.

Even Judas seemed impressed.

Ava stilled long enough to lean forward, take a draw of her drink, and then open her mouth to fire off a few more.

"Whoa there, firecracker." Nero lifted his hand, stilling her words. "Let Mor speak."

They wanted to know it all, every juicy detail. I could see what juicy details the Wolves were interested in.

"Tell us *everything*." Ava glared at the Wolves and asked anyway. "What's his name?"

God, how was I going to say it with a straight face. "Funny thing..." I totally stole her line. "I, ah, didn't quite get it."

They all stared at me, until I shrunk in my seat.

"You didn't get it?" Ava muttered. "You didn't get what? *Anything?*"

I motioned my head toward the mammoth thing on the end of the table. "I got a book."

Bond just snarled, as Judas leaned backwards. None of them believed me...*none of them*.

I leaned forward, grasped the bloodshake waiting for me and pressed my lips to the straw. Mutters broke out before the Wolves retreated to their seats once more. I glanced around the rest of the dining hall catching Nesrin and the others staring.

Everyone stared now, and it wasn't just hateful glances and the rolling of eyes. It was an *uncomfortable* stare, like they just didn't know where they stood.

Welcome to my fucking life.

At least they all had each other, who did I have? I glanced at Ava, who watched me from the corner of her eye and slipped smoked salmon into her mouth. I didn't know how to tell her about the Ancient, and I sure as hell didn't know how to explain my new teacher.

Nefarious Leathers. I couldn't even say his damn name without laughing.

The bell rang for the next class and I finished my shake,

grabbed this anvil of a book and hauled it to Psychic 101. I tried to avoid my friends' questions for the rest of the day, and laughed a little too loud at their jokes. Mr. Jacobsen just looked at me like I was weird and continued with the six myths about fragmented realities, until finally the last bell rang.

"Thank the Ancient," I muttered and shoved up from my chair.

I slung my pack over my shoulder, grabbed the book, and headed for the doorway. But no footsteps followed behind me, not like they had before. I glanced at Ava and the Wolves as they hung back, watching me.

"I'll catch you later," Judas muttered.

He was talking to me... "Oh, okay, sure."

It smarted. I wasn't going to lie, but I should've expected it, after all it was me shutting them out, wasn't it? My head was a jumbled mess and the sense of unease seemed to grow. My cheeks were burning by the time I got to the dorm. I shoved through the door, stormed across the foyer and then climbed the stairs. My arms were aching when I shoved the key into the lock and stumbled into my room.

I dropped the massive book onto the end of the bed and the thing bounced before the mattress sank under its weight. I could hear Ava fussing in her room as I closed my door and headed for the bathroom.

I used the bathroom, washed my hands and my face. "You're an idiot," I muttered to myself in the mirror. "A real tossbag." And then I yanked open my wardrobe and changed my clothes.

I waited for the knock on my door, or even for the damn thing to fly open before Ava barged in. But it never came, and my world grew a little less *vibrant*. There was a groan of a chair from somewhere outside the room. I cracked open the door and peered out, watching Ava haul the sofa around the foyer floor before slumping onto it and crossing her ankles and opening a text book.

Things must be bad if she was doing actual work.

I sucked in a hard breath and stepped out, casually making my way down to her. She pretended not to notice and I pretended not to notice her not noticing me.

"Whatcha reading?" I glanced to the other students outside, some were peering into the tree line as though they expected a little fluffy beast to launch out any moment.

Ava's only response was to glare at the page even harder. Our first disagreement, and it was all my fault. Fucking awesome. I turned and dropped into the sofa beside her. "Look, I'm sorry."

She shook her head and gave a shrug. "It's okay. You gotta do what you gotta do, right?"

"It's just," I started and then stopped. "You wouldn't understand."

"Oh, so now I'm not in your league? Wow, I didn't realize being an Understudy meant you were suddenly too good for the rest of us. And all it took was one private class."

My heart sank. "That's not what I meant and you know it."

"Really? Then by all means, tell me what you meant."

God, she was going to make me tell her. "It's just...my teacher, and the Ancient. They're not...not what you think. They're...*strange*.."

She jerked her gaze toward me, one brow rising. Even if I was an outright cow by hiding things she was ready to be my best friend in an instant. "Tell me everything, leaving nothing out."

I sucked in a breath. "His name is Nefarious Leathers."

There was stunned silence.

You could hear a demonic bunny fart.

"Nefarious *Leathers?*" she muttered.

I just nodded.

The *hmpf...hmpfhmpf...hmpf* turned into hard, jerking sobs until with a sudden roar I realized they weren't sobs at all. But laughter. Ava howled hysterically. *"Oww,"* she grabbed hold of her stomach and gasped for a breath. *"N-Nefarious...L...Leathers?"*

Her eyes watered. Tears slid down her face.

She seemed to pool from the sofa and spill to the floor.

Her body was shaking and trembling and I was unable to do anything but watch her...until my stomach started to quake and that tremor raced. A giggle slipped free and moved deeper shaking loose the fist clenched around me.

"Oh my God." Ava giggled. "That name...no wonder you didn't want to tell us."

"It's not just the name," I sniggered and leaned close to murmur. "The Ancient is a cross-dresser."

She stopped dead, eyes widened. "No...freaking...way."

I nodded. "I shit you not. He orders takeout, which I have to run and get for him. Loves leather, and he said the best thing about being a Vampire is that everyone thinks he's sexy."

"Sure, if you're blind...the dude is practically a fossil." She sniggered and shook her head. "He's got skin," she lifted her arm and pinched the underside of her arm and then moved her hand about five inches lower. "To here."

I sniggered and shook my head.

"Reminds me of those dogs, you know the one with all the rolls, they're cute and all. *But sexy?*" She was all in now. One million percent hooked. "You have to tell me *everything*. Leave nothing out."

And I told her...all the craziness...all the bizarre; and the doubt and darkness slipped away. We were best friends again, laughing with tangling legs, falling into each other as we giggled and Ava snorted, which only made us laugh harder.

"Oh man." She shoved a fist against her belly and tried to breathe.

And everything was right in my world once more.

"So, what are you going to do about Leathers?" She finally came around to it. "He's hot, right?"

"So not my type," I murmured.

"No fur?" She gave me a wink.

The words lingered as Judas, Bond and Nero filled my mind. "No, I guess not."

"Holy shit, I can't believe you've got three guys interested in you."

"Me neither," I murmured.

But it didn't feel anything but easy, like they were all one perfect happy memory, and yet they were individual, each with their own drives. I wanted to know more about them, each of them. I unfurled my limbs from around hers and shoved from the sofa. "They said something about milkshakes and brownies."

"You go ahead," she murmured. "I'm just gonna kick back here and relax."

"You sure?" I cocked my head. "Not like you to pass up something like that."

"Go." She shooed me away with a flick of her hand. "But bring me back a piece of brownie, those things are delicious."

I laughed and headed for the door. "I'll bring you back two. I know how you haunt the damn vending machines at midnight."

"Do not," she snarled.

But there was one person she couldn't lie too...and it seemed that went both ways.

I strode out of my dorm and headed for theirs. Memories slipped in from last semester, darkened basements and dead bodies, and a ploy to kill my father as we celebrated my 100th birthday. So much had changed, but many things hadn't...many things had just evolved, and as I reached the front door to their dorm, I couldn't help but smile.

Voices spilled out as I yanked open the dorm door and stepped inside. I made my way toward their doors, tried the handles and found them locked. I knocked on each door, drawing the gaze of a demon who lingered in the shadows, but there was no answer. I turned away and made for the front door once more. They must be already there, waiting for me.

My steps were hurried now as I raced for the main building. I thought I'd get sick of this place, that I'd grow bored with the classes and exhausted from the other students. But I wasn't, if anything I was excited to see Judas and the guys. The sky was darkening as I entered the main building and made my way to the cafeteria.

The dull roar of voices filled the hallway, excitement mingled with terror.

"A goddamn rabbit." I heard someone say and turned my head.

A guy from my class was motioning in the air how he had to climb a tree to save his life. He lifted his head as I neared, and our gaze connected. I bit the insides of my cheeks, fighting to stop from smiling and strode into the dining hall.

The place was packed. Nesrin and her friends taking up their familiar post. I turned for Judas' table and found it invaded by others. My steps stilled. I scanned the rest of the hall, searching every face, and every gaze.

But they weren't here...I turned, checking the corners behind me and felt the heavy weight of stares settle. I didn't need to look to know who it was, so I left, leaving Nesrin and her watchful gaze behind.

Dusky pinks deepened to red against the horizon, stretching out as far as I could see as I strode toward my dorm. I shoved through the door and caught Ava lower her book. "You forgot my brownie."

"Huh?" I lifted my head.

"My brownie... Hey, what's wrong?" She sat up straighter, closing the book.

"The Wolves weren't there. I dunno, maybe I got my signals crossed. Maybe I went too late. I thought...I thought they wanted to..."

"That's okay, we can hang out. There's a Vampire movie on later if you want to watch it? Queen of the Damned?"

I shook my head. "It's okay, maybe next time. I think I'm just going to read a book in bed and turn in early."

She just nodded, watching as I made my way to upstairs my room. Maybe I'd got this all wrong...maybe the friend zone with Judas and his pack was just where we were meant to stay. I slipped into my room, hit the lights and headed for the shower.

I lost my thoughts amongst the hot spray on my back. It wasn't the cascading water from my shower back home, but the heat was enough to soothe the twinge of disappointment. I stepped out, dried myself and slipped on something cotton and warm. Faint howls echoed through the night air. I dragged a brush through my hair and walked to the balcony.

The moon was full and low in the sky. I drew in the cool air and felt life in my lungs as I stretched my fingers stretched overhead. In this moment, it felt like I could almost touch the silver rays.

A sharp howl ripped through the night, closer, making me flinch and draw my hands in. A flash of white scurried from the dark woods.

On a night of the full moon, the Beasts were out to play.

I switched on the small desk lamp and turned off the overhead lights before climbing into bed.

Nefarious Leathers...the Ancient...the Wolves. They haunted me as I opened the cover of this big ass book and scanned the Latin. *Necronomicon...the book of the Dead...*

The words had power, spelled pages stole me away, I flicked through one after another, losing track of time until the pale silver touch of the moon pulled away.

Sleep called. I closed the book, and shoved the heavy thing to the edge of the bed before I switched off the light.

Laughter echoed somewhere in the distance as I closed my eyes. I sank into the darkness, and was ripped away from the worries of this world...returning instead to the night of my party, where the champagne glasses clinked and darkness waited with bared fangs.

Nails clawed against the window in my dream...*scratch...scratch...scratch...scratch...*

I brushed the hand away... Stop it. Stop making that sound.

Scratch...scratch....scratch...

The squeal of nails on glass was piercing. I thrashed, rising to the surface and turning over.

Scratch.

I wrenched open my eyes and stilled. That sound...that sound wasn't in my dream.

Scraaatttcchhhh.

I shoved up from my bed. "Goddamn Wolves...playing hard to get and then wake me in the middle of the damn night."

Anger lashed inside me as I strode to the balcony doors, twisted the handle and then yanked. Darkness tumbled inside with a whimper. I reached out, grasping the body as a creature fell into my arms.

"Please..." the creature of midnight whispered and lifted iridescent orange eyes to mine. "Morwenna Livingstone please help me."

CHAPTER FOUR

ALL THAT GLITTERS ISN'T GOLD

THE SILVERY HUE OF THE MOON CLUNG TO THE creature. Tiny white fangs glinted, protruding below its lip as it whispered, "I'm sorry to intrude. Is it okay if I...if I come in?"

I caught the familiar whiff of old blood on cold breath as I held him, my fingers touching nothing more than skin and bone.

"Come in. Are you hurt?" I stumbled into the room and collapsed against the mattress. "Is someone chasing you?"

Faint howls clung to the night. The beasts were outside, still hunting.

Chuck, I should get Chuck. I reached for my phone, fingers dancing across the screen for his name.

"Morwenna," the Vampire creature whispered, drawing my focus to him.

His amber eyes were like lights pinned in the darkness. Thin lips, a long nose, and pasty skin. He sat, hunched, a small hump curling over his back.

"How do you know my name?" It was too dark to study

his expression, so I crouched in front of him. "Tell me what's going on?"

He shook his head, the hood sliding off his head, revealing shaggy hair. "I had to come and see you. It's important."

Thoughts spun in my mind. I gripped his arm, so bony I feared it might shatter if I squeezed too hard. "Talk to me."

A tiny pink tongue skirted pale lips. "A glass of water, please. I'm thirsty."

I jumped to my feet, crossed the room and flipped on the bathroom light. "You don't have to be afraid," I called. "No one's going to hurt you here."

Thoughts raced as I grabbed a glass from the shelf above the basin, dumped my toothbrush and toothpaste into the sink before I rinsed the tumbler.

A steady stream of water hit the bottom of the glass. I filled it to the top and switched it off.

"Do you know my Dad?" I strode from the bathroom, glass in hand, and then stopped in the middle of my room. "Hello?"

The room was empty. Curtains flapping...but the creature was gone.

Like he'd never been here at all.

"Okay, that's freaking weird." I lifted the glass to my lips and drank the water, before I took a tentative step toward the balcony.

"Hey, little Vamp...where are you?" I called softly.

There was no sign of him, and down below only shadows gathered in the grounds.

Distant howls shattered the quiet. I stepped inside and locked the glass door. "You wake me, get me all worried and then take off," I muttered, heading through my room to check the hallway. Nothing. The only sound was Ava's snores in the room next to mine. The Kraken sounded like a damn bear.

"What would make you run like that?"

But there was nothing out here, nothing but shadows and quiet. I turned back to my room and stepped inside before locking the door.

The closet was clean, all my designer clothes still in plastic wrap.

Darkness descended as I hit the switch. I headed for my bed, kicked something soft and felt it tumble. Shit. The pile of clothes I meant to put away. I'd clean it tomorrow. Tonight, I needed sleep. I'd deal with everything else in the morning.

The creature lingered inside my head as I closed my eyes. Chuck would know what it had been about. The Vamp knew almost everything, including how to be an overbearing pain in my ass. I rolled over, drawing the blanket to my chin and closed my eyes. Sleep came fast.

BLINDING light speared through my lids. I cracked open my eyes to the glare. "What the fuck!" I squinted against the brightness. "Helene turn off the light!"

But there was no response. I pushed my legs out of bed and pulled myself upright, rubbing my eyes. There was no Helene...no, anyone, actually. Just the light, piercing like the midday sun without my sacred ring for protection. I wrenched my hand high, covering my eyes. Why the heck was it so bright?

But the light didn't just bore into me...it almost...danced.

I blinked, my eyes adjusting to the sparkle and turned to my bedside table.

The surface was studded with hundreds of precious

stones. Sunlight glinted on the edges, throwing multi-colored light in every direction. What the hell? I reached over, my fingers sinking into the brilliance only to find my bed shimmered and sparkled underneath me.

They were everywhere.

The walls. The floor. The ceiling, and the furniture, even my damn phone shone—made of jewels. "What the fuck. This is so weird."

Panic crept along my spine as my bare feet touched the gems.

I stepped toward the door, ready to leave this room behind. But there was no handle, and there was no key. I lifted my head, searching sparkling wardrobes, and star studded walls.

"Ava!" I called. "Ava, I need your help!"

The balcony. I turned to the curtain now heavy and stuck, weighed down with jewels. I stepped outside to find the jewels had taken over the landscape too. The lawn, the trees, branches dripping with enormous red rubies.

"Holy fuck, the school morphed into the Bejeweled game."

I moved to the edge of my balcony and stared into the darkness of Ava's room. "Ava...Ava can you hear me?"

"No, she can't." A deep, guttural snarl came from behind me, before the voice whispered next to my ear. "Careful Vampire... You just might lose your head."

Instinct kicked in. Fangs grew over my lips as I spun, fists curled, ready to lash out.

But my world whirled with me, so fast, I stumbled and then fell.

A SCREAM RIPPED free as I woke with a jolt. I stared at the

end of my bed as the sun's morning rays spilled in between the gaps of the curtains. Just a dream. Just a crazy, goddamn dream. I slumped backwards, my head bouncing as it hit the pillow.

"Goddamn. What the hell was in the blood I drank last night?"

Whatever it was, it was trippy.

Classes. Wolves, Ava...my class with goddamn Leathers. I groaned and kicked the sheets from my body and then rolled. I slid my feet from the bed and stepped on the mess of half folded clothes. The memory of the Vamp creature came back to me.

Maybe that was just part of the dream. God knows it was all crazy enough.

Weird creatures. Visits in the middle of the night.

Careful Vampire...you just might lose your head.

I spun with the echo, my heart hammering, and searched the room. Nothing there, okay? Not a fucking thing. I hurried toward the bathroom, carving through the pile of clothes and kicked something...*hard.*

Agony shot up my foot like a jolt of electricity. I wailed, collapsing half onto my bed and slid to the floor as I grabbed my ankle. "For the love of a goat nut. Fuck!"

I curled in on myself, rolling back and forth until the pain eased. Tears welled in my eyes. I pawed through the clothes, found the corner of the bedframe and then something soft.

"What the Hell?" I groped the bag, finding the strings which drew the end tight and forgot all about my pain for a second.

It was a bag...a purple bag not much bigger than my fist, but something clinked and jumped inside. "Where the hell did you come from?"

I shoved against the floor with one foot and hobbled to my desk before I sank into the seat. My entire toe pulsed with pain.

But the agony wasn't all that consumed me...it was the bag. I twisted the thing in my hand, finding a sigil sewn into one side. An upside down triangle with the ends curling outward, and a V at the base, crossing over the curls. I ran a finger over the pattern, one I'd never seen before, and knew what it was...it was a Witch's sigil.

A sharp shot of energy zapped through my finger. I jolted in my seat, knocked backwards, the chair rocking with me.

"Oww!" The tip of my index finger burned red before the pain eased. I limped to the bathroom and stuck my hand under running water.

What in the world?

I dabbed the burn with my towel and glanced at the bag. *Don't touch it.* The words filled me. But the dream haunted me...the damn dream, more than some freaking blood-spiked trip. It almost felt like a...*prophecy.*

Like it'd all been real.

The little creature in the middle of the night.

The sparkling—I took a step, crossing my bedroom—perfect, jewels. I reached for the tie strings, touching at first. This time where was no stinging burn...this time there was only a *throb...throb...throb*...like the bag had a pulse of its own.

I opened the string and looked inside.

Something sparkled. Something glinted.

I tipped the bag, watching as diamonds spilled from inside the pouch. Tens of them...*hundreds of them,* glinted from the morning sun, crashing light through my room in the most dazzling rays.

I plucked one from the pile, holding it between my fingers. A tremor hummed against my skin, making me drop the stone and stumble backward out of my chair. Without looking back, I headed out of my room and banged on Ava's door.

She opened it, still in her pyjama dress with tiny mermaids on it. Adorable. Her blonde hair stuck outward, and she slouched.

"This better be life or death, or I'm going all Kraken on your ass." She rubbed sleep out of her eyes.

I grabbed her wrist. "You need to see this. Now."

"What is it?"

"You'll see." I dragged her into my room and closed the door behind us.

She glanced around the place. "Okay, so your room is a pigsty. Oh, and you're planning on getting a goldfish for a pet?"

"What are you talking about?"

"The clear stones." She pointed to the table. "I used to have those at home for the tank where I kept my pet crab."

"Ava, those are diamonds." And I let loose a long rant about the night's events, my dream, and this bag that almost ripped off my pinkie toe.

"No fucking way!" She raced to the table and picked up a handful, staring at them. "Do you think they're real?"

"I doubt some hunchback Vamp would visit me to give me fake ones."

"Shit." She flopped into my seat, staring at her open palm. "They're beautiful."

When she reached for the bag, I called out, "Careful."

She flinched, grasping the purple bag, her fingers tracing the sigil stitched into the front of the bag.

"Doesn't that burn?"

Shaking her head, she scooped all the stones back inside and tied it up. "Did you know that some diamonds were formed in outer space. And apparently, they're found in the mines in Africa and South America, after being deposited by an asteroid that collided with earth. So, these could be alien diamonds. What if they are more valuable and someone is trying to set you up? Wouldn't be the first time."

"How do you even know about the space stuff?"

She glanced up at me, one eyebrow arching higher than the other. "I read articles online. You ought to try it sometime."

"Not everything online is real." Like the lies I'd read on Vamp Daily about my family. We never sacrificed humans in our backyard. We weren't savages. We got blood delivered by a courier. "Anyway, what am I meant to do with the stones? Maybe I just hand them over to Chuck."

"No," she blurted and dumped the tied bag on the table. "As much as it pains me to say so, last time you told Chuck anything, it caused a world of troubles. We hand it over to Principal Stone. It's her campus and she can take care of it."

The suggestion made sense, except that hunchback Vamp knew my full name and then I was there in that strange dream. But I didn't want problems, so I nodded. "Let's hand them over to her."

"Perfect." She turned toward the door. "I'll be back in two hours after more sleep and at a more reasonable time."

My mouth opened to call her back, to get this done now, but she'd already vanished into the hallway and shut the door behind her.

I glanced back at the bag of diamonds, the instinct in my gut churning. I stared at the top of my finger, bright red from the burn. What exactly did this mean?

CHAPTER FIVE

WHERE THERE'S SMOKE THERE'S USUALLY MR. LEATHERS

Homecoming Black and White Ball. The posters were everywhere.

"What are you going as, for the school dance?" Ava murmured and shoved the last chunk of muesli bar into her mouth.

I turned and looked at her with one brow raised. "You know for someone enlightened with all the mysteries of the universe, you sure are a little thick sometimes."

"What?" she muttered. "I thought you might want to change it up, from the normal, stuck-up pain in the ass you usually are."

I lifted my hand and flipped her the bird.

"Anyway." She ignored the motion, just as she always did. "I guess the real question is, which one are you going to go with?"

"Which one *what*? I have no idea what you mean." I muttered staring at the hallway as Judas, Bond, and Nero lifted their gazes toward me. Energy flared through my chest.

"The dance. The Wolves? *Duh.*"

I had more than the damn dance on my mind. "I don't know. But what I do know is I need to figure this out."

"Maybe we could cash them in? Buy a damn island." Ava murmured.

"No way." My hand dropped to the diamonds in my pocket. "Not gonna happen, not until we work this out."

"We?" she muttered. "I swear if I have to eat someone...or *anyone,* again, I'm cutting off the friendship."

"What about Chuck?" I threw back with a sneer. "You cut off the friendship and he comes with me."

She stopped dead in the middle of the hall. "You wouldn't..."

"Oh, I would." I smiled. "I most certainly would. So you, my kickass, snores like a damn truck driver, best friend, are helping me figure this out."

I caught a scent, someone masculine and *canine.*

"Figure what out?" Judas murmured in front of me. Bond and Nero stood on either side. It was always the way with them.

Judas didn't glance at Ava, only held my gaze, searching for something.

"I missed you at the cafeteria last night," I murmured, wanting him to know I'd turned up, even if he didn't.

"Didn't think you'd want to go after such an exhaustive first class with that tattooed dip-shit for a teacher," he snarled, those brooding dark eyes glinted as the other Wolves turned to their Alpha.

"That's *Leathers,* to you." Ava stepped up and glared at Judas...well, tried to anyway. "Mr. *Nefarious Leathers.*"

Judas flinched and turned to her. "You've got to be shitting me, right?"

I sighed at the smile on her lips and groaned inwardly. "Okay, *okay...it's hilarious, I get it.*"

"Nefarious Leathers," Bond murmured, and Nero chuckled.

"That's your competition, buddy." Ava giggled and lifted a hand, poking Judas in the center of his chest.

"There's no competition," I teased.

"Damn right there isn't," Judas murmured and seized my gaze. "Not from him...or anyone for that matter."

"I'm gonna leave you guys right there." Ava blew me a kiss and then strode away.

She loved throwing bombs before she left. It was starting to become her favorite past time.

"Now, getting back to the question, what are you and Ava up to this time, and what needs *'figuring out'*." He hooked his fingers in the air with the quotation marks.

I glanced to the others. I'd trusted them with my life...twice, and they'd not let me down, so why did this feel different? Why did this feel like I was handing over a lot more than a bag of priceless jewels?

Because it's what they want you to think. The words filled me.

The warning voice behind me in the dream was resurrected, sending goosebumps along my skin. I had to do something...I had to trust someone—I lifted my gaze. I'd trust them. I took a step closer, watching as Judas's nostrils flared, and the other two moved in.

I lowered my voice and dropped my head, speaking into the side of his neck—Hell he smelled good, like the full moon rising, like the perfume of night jasmine still clinging to his skin. "Last night someone came to my balcony."

I felt all three Wolves stiffen.

"It was some kind of Vampire creature. He looked frightened, like someone was chasing him. He asked if he could come in."

Brown eyes seized mine as Judas turned to me. All I could see were those lips…those perfect lips.

"Yes," I whispered. "I let him in."

"You really need to brush up on your own kind," Bond muttered, watching me as I stared at Judas' mouth. "Just sayin'."

"Anyway." I shook myself from the trance. "I bought him in, he asked for a glass of water and when I came back he was gone, vanished like he'd never been there at all. I searched the hall, and then went back to bed and had the craziest ass dream imaginable. My room was filled with diamonds."

Other students rushed past us.

"*Kiki!* No running in the hallways, please!" A male teacher cried out as he passed. He cut us a glare. "Shouldn't you four be getting to class?"

"Yes, Mr. May," Nero answered but didn't move a muscle. "We should."

The teacher just looked at us and then kept on walking, muttering under his breath about *cocky Wolves.*

"And?" Judas murmured.

The words caught in the back of my throat. I couldn't say them, so I reached out, grasped Judas' hand in mine and slipped it into the pocket of my jacket.

His chest rose with a hard breath, something predatory sparkled in his eyes, and for a second, I thought he felt it…felt that raw, *hunger* from the diamonds like I had, until he closed his fist around the bag in my pocket and the jewels clattered and clinked.

"They were real, *all* real. The creature must've left them in my room before he disappeared."

Judas slipped his hand from mine.

"There's a sigil on the bag, that's what I needed help

figuring out," I murmured as the shrill sound of the class bell rang along the hallway.

Judas just stared into my eyes and then nodded. "Then we'll all help, but no more letting crazy ass creatures into you room at night, okay? Especially the Vampire kind."

I nodded. But for a second, I thought we were talking about two very different Vampires.

"Right, let's go to the Dens and Dives class. Ms. Truro isn't going to wait for everyone," Nero pipped in.

They turned and we walked to class together, slipping into the room as the teacher stared.

"Nice of you to join us," she snarled and then with a wave of her hand, slammed the door.

We didn't have many Witches at Bestias Academy, and the ones we did have were snarling and short fused. I slipped into the seat between Ava and Judas, while the other Wolves took one seat up from the Alpha and one down.

We turned our focus to the white board where the map of Tricks City was divided between the races.

"Right, class. Today we're learning about the division of breeds, what that means to the races of the future, and of the past."

"The future is fangs!" someone called out.

"Yes, yes," Ms. Truro muttered and waved her hand, a ripple of magic pricked my skin.

There was a muffled mutter and a scrape of the chair. I turned and glanced at the loud-mouth who'd spoken out of turn and caught the wide eyed stare of a Vampire with his mouth sewn shut. It looked a tiny bit painful. Hell, this teacher wasn't messing around.

"The future in this class." Ms. Truro leaned on her desk

and glared at each one of us. "Is respect. Do I make myself clear?"

"Yes, Ms. Truro," I mouthed the words as the entire class turned quiet and still.

"Now, that's better..." She pushed off the desk and gave a wave of her hand, hard gasps echoed from the Vamp behind us. "As I was saying...division of breeds...."

We never spoke another word in the class. Only watched the screen as the lines through Tricks City brightened and dulled.

But she had a point, and I wasn't talking about the loud-mouthed Vamp who wanted to see our kind rule all the races. I was talking about the future...a future that I was a big part of.

We opened our books and took notes. For a Witch, she had a lot of insight into the migration of our kind into the masses of mortals, and left me with a lot of questions when the bell rang once more.

"You seeing Mr. *Leathers* next?" Judas whispered after class.

"Yes, and don't be getting all snarly. I'm totally not interested in him." There was a grumble and a snarl from Judas, before I stilled and then turned. "I know. Come with me."

"What?"

I reached for his hand once more, and this time I slipped my fingers between his. "Come with me to class."

Bond's brow rose. Nero cocked his head. "Do it," the blue eyed Wolf murmured. "We'll take notes, you won't miss a thing."

Judas glanced at me, and I gave a shrug. "It's up to you."

The bell rang overhead again and both Bond and Nero took a step backwards, then another, leaving Judas behind.

"Okay," the Alpha murmured. "I'll come."

I tugged his hand, leading him to the classroom I used for Ancient studies and pushed through the door.

Nefarious leaned against his desk, his legs crossed in front of him as he read an open book in his hand. He lifted his head as I strode through tugging Judas behind me.

"Ah, I was wondering when the boyfriend was going to turn up." He glanced at Judas and smiled.

"Oh, Judas isn't really my...." I cut him a glance and caught him wince. "Oh, ummm...Judas is a really good friend."

"Sure, welcome anyway." The teacher stood, took a step toward the Alpha, and reached out his hand. "Nefarious Leathers."

"Judas Blackthorne."

"Ah, the infamous Blackthorne Wolves, no wonder." Mr. Leathers cut me a glance.

I waited, glancing from one to another like I was waiting for the punchline to the joke. "What is that supposed to mean?"

"Nothing," Judas murmured. 'You'd better...." He motioned to the seat in the middle of the room. Intrigue filled me. My father kept all mention of the Wolves from me growing up. I'd never heard about the Blackthorne family, let alone anything else.

"Right, I thought today we'd start with you."

I flinched. "Me?"

Nefarious slid the open book onto the desk. "Yes, you. I mean you must've wondered...why, you, right?"

Judas slipped into the seat at the edge of the room, leaving me in the firing line.

"Why me, what?"

There was a shake of the Vampire's head as he crossed

the distance. Leather pants shone under the lights. Today he wasn't wearing a cut-off shirt that showed his tattoos, but instead a mesh shirt that showed everything else.

My cheeks grew warm as I looked away. *Why me...why me....*

Why not you? That dark warning voice from my dream slipped into my head.

"I mean, you must've given it at least a little thought. The role of the Understudy hasn't been handed out in almost a thousand years. Haven't you been curious about the previous occupant of that role, the Great Elysian?"

I could feel Judas' eyes on me, feel that heaviness as I shook my head.

"Morwenna, you really need to start to look at yourself, and not as this love-struck teenager. Look at who you are as a Vampire. Your abilities, your power."

"Lack of abilities, you mean." I lifted my gaze and felt that burn in my cheeks consume me. "You know you're right. I have wondered why me, I mean, I suck at drinking blood from a vein. I'm decent at hunting, although I hate it."

The teacher just rested against the desk again and shook his head. "You really don't get it, do you? I mean, I knew I was getting a diamond in the rough, but a clueless diamond, now that's something."

Diamond. He said the word. Was it code for something? Did he know about the creature...did he set this whole thing up? I shot a glance toward Judas.

"Stand up for a moment, if you will."

Judas just stared, clueless, while I clenched my jaw and jerked my head toward Leathers. But Judas was no damn help, sitting back against his seat as I rose from mine.

Nefarious stepped between the rows of empty seats and

stopped in front of me. "I'm going to touch you, is that okay? Just placing my hands on your shoulders, that's all."

I cringed inside but nodded slowly. He held my gaze, took a slow, hard breath, trying to ready himself and then murmured. "Here goes nothing."

His fingers clenched around my shoulders, his eyes seemed to bore into mine. I waited...and waited...*and waited*. There were no fireworks, no blinding light of reality to sweep me off my feet. If anything, there was this gnawing feeling of being uncomfortable...like he was drawing me closer.

Blue eyes beckoned, Mr. Leathers hands seemed to slide down my arms, even though they never moved. Warmth spilled from my side, and crept into my chest.

Nefarious' lips parted, black pupils swallowed the blue. The white tips of fangs peeked out from under red lips. *Do you understand now?* He murmured without moving his lips. *Do you see...why you?*

I shook my head as the warmth rose inside me. Sparkling light filled my mind, a remnant from the dream. The diamonds. I lowered my hand to my pocket and slipped my fingers inside. But there was no heat, not even a trace of warmth. But the feeling swelled inside me, like a tiny lick of fire that raced through my body.

"You are meant for something bigger than all this," Mr. Leathers murmured. "And you draw almost everyone into you. I felt it the moment I saw you...and I know the Ancient did as well."

"I never met him before my party. But I felt him, his power raced through me, it was like..."

"Like you were on fire. But the most beautiful fire, like liquid sunlight filled your veins and you swallowed it down, unable to get enough."

I jerked my gaze toward him. "Yes."

"You didn't need to," my teacher explained. "He met you, just as we all met you. Have you ever heard of a Transcendent?"

I shook my head as he lifted a hand from my shoulder and brushed away a strand of hair from my face. "You, my dear Understudy, will be one of the most powerful Vampires in history, mark my words."

He stepped away, leaving me to falter in that burning desire that raced through my veins. "What...what did you do to me?"

"Nothing that wasn't already waiting to be unlocked...I just showed you the path to unlock it, that's all."

Power trembled over my fingers and spilled out. I closed my eyes as the desk next to me vibrated, and the feeling swelled, consuming the room like wildfire.

"That's it," Nefarious murmured. "That's it, right there."

I jerked open my eyes and wrenched my gaze to Judas. Awe, fear and conflict filled his brown eyes.

Nefarious just shook his head. "You honestly didn't think you were just any other Vampire, surely."

And in an instant the fire was gone.

That was the thing...*I* *did.* I was the daughter of a famous Vampire, the one who stood in the shadows...the one who did what I was told. I was the one who stood still while the world around me spun. "Yes," I murmured. "Yes, I did."

"Then you, Understudy, have a lot to learn."

The bell chimed overhead. It felt like seconds had passed. I looked at the clock above the wall...it'd been hours.

"Look transcendence up in the book I gave you." Nefarious stepped around the side of his desk. "I think it'll make some interesting reading. I look forward to hearing your thoughts on the matter."

And just like that I was dismissed. Judas climbed to his feet as Nefarious yanked the open book closer and continued reading as though the lesson that'd just rocked my world had been nothing more than an inconvenience.

I scowled and opened my mouth to say something but Judas gripped my elbow and steered me toward the door. Voices filled my head as students chattered and giggled, most of them making their way to the cafeteria.

"I want to go back in there." I glanced at the door as Judas closed it behind him.

"Why?"

"Because, I... *Because.*"

"Because what he said was the truth?" Judas' hand never left my elbow.

I lifted my gaze to his. "You don't really believe any of that, do you?"

He just chuckled and shook his head. "Mor, I think the only one who *doesn't* believe it is you."

And then he dropped his hand and strode away. I raced to catch up as Judas slipped between the other students and worked his way to the table where the rest of the gang waited.

I smiled, muttered "excuse me," and followed.

He was already sitting by the time I got there. I glanced at Ava, and the bloodshake waiting for me and leaned across the table towards Judas. "No, I don't and I don't think you should either."

"Shouldn't what?" Ava cut in.

Bond and Nero glanced at the Alpha and waited for my answer.

"It seems Mor here doesn't like the fact that she's unlike every other Vampire." Judas laid it all out on the table.

"Why's that?" Bond looked to me for the answer.

"Because I'm not..." I tried to make them understand. "Don't you think I'd know the difference...I mean, my entire family are Vampires."

"And ours are Wolves," Nero added. "But some in our pack are well, just different."

"I'm eating." Bond stood and then looked at Judas, "You?"

There was a shake of his head. "I'm good. I'm just going to sit here and watch Mor wrestle with her conscience for a while."

I wanted to flip *him* the bird, but instead I just stared at him, and then turned to Ava who picked at the edges of a brownie. "Tell him."

"Tell him what?" She chewed and swallowed before taking a sip of her milkshake.

"Tell him I'm normal."

She gave a shrug, "Normal is overrated in my opinion. Take it from me."

I stilled, and then gripped the bottom of my black glass bloodshake and pulled it close. Ava was different...I glanced around the others. I'd never heard of a Kraken shifter before, let alone met one. She seemed to be handling the fact okay.

"Just drink your shake, Mor," Ava murmured.

I sucked on the straw, and drank my meal while Bond and Nero came back.

"You wanted to go to the library?" Judas watched me drink.

"You told them?" Ava whispered.

"I couldn't shut them out, could I?"

"Just give me a sec." Bond heaped spoonfuls of mashed potato and gravy into his mouth and Nero consumed a steak in three massive bites.

Judas stood as Ava devoured the last bite of her brownie and sucked her shake dry. I followed, gulping and then glanced at Bond pushing to stand once more. "It's okay, you can catch up."

"Nope." He grabbed the bone of the biggest shank I'd ever seen and pushed to stand. "I can eat on the way."

I grabbed the glasses and the plates, piling them at the end of the table before we headed for the hallway. I had a lot to think about, and this...*Transcendence* was just the icing on a never ending cake.

We made for the front of the building, pushed through the door and headed for the Lodge. Students milled around on the grassy area, sitting in the sun. But most were inside, leaving us the only ones on the footpath as it curled near the wooded area.

"So, tell me what we're actually looking for," Bond walked, chewed, and talked.

I grabbed the bag from my pocket and raised my hand, pointing at the sigil sewn into the bag. "Well, we can start with that."

A small, pale blur scurried from the trees and stopped dead in the middle of the pavement. It was a bunny, but...it'd changed. No longer cute and fluffy. This creature had blood red eyes, and hideous razored fangs. The thing hissed and lunged for Bond who dropped the hunk of meat in his hand.

It hit the ground with a *thud,* before the demonic rabbit scurried forward, sank those hideous fangs into the shank and dragged the meal backwards into the tree line.

We all watched, unable to take our eyes off the damn thing.

"I was enjoying that," Bond muttered and sighed.

Ava turned to look at me...and the Wolves followed one by one.

It seemed our bunnies were growing bolder by the day. Crap.

Hell knew what was next.

CHAPTER SIX

RABBITS TURNED RABID

Row after row of books lined the shelves. Everything was sorted alphabetically, and there were three floors that looked identical.

A muffled stillness wove around me as I walked down an aisle, my fingers running over the spines facing outward. Everything I could ever want to know about emblems sat here. History, creation, races, and even how to make your own. The five of us split up, each taking various topics to research the icon on the bag of diamonds. We'd been here a couple of hours already with no clue on where the sigil on the bag of diamonds came from.

Movement from the next row caught my attention and I peered through the gaps in the shelving to see Bond casually plucking out random books, his back to me. He looked over his shoulder at me as if sensing me and winked. The dimple in his cheek that appeared when he smiled was so devilishly divine. He had such deep eyes, revealing his Wolf side, but he had the kind of strong face I could admire for hours—so gorgeous. I suddenly forgot how to breathe. Then he walked away. Ava was correct, whenever the Wolves were in my company, I seemed to lose myself.

I shook my head, needing to focus, then studied the books under my hand when the word 'Vampire' caught my attention and I drew the volume out. A small puff of dust tickled my nose, and I flipped the book open to find rows and rows of tiny text. With a sigh, I flicked through the pages for any illustrations of emblems. Focusing seemed impossible when I kept thinking back to my last class with Mr. Leathers. The power I'd sensed inside me, how he spoke directly into my thoughts, and the energy in my veins was like nothing I'd experienced before.

How had he tapped into it when I'd never been able to? Why hadn't Dad told me, or didn't he know? And he claimed I was the most powerful Vampire.

I chuckled under my breath. As if.

Footsteps closed in ahead of me, and I glanced up to find Judas strolling toward me, his hands stuffed into the pockets of black school pants that hung low on his hips, his untucked, button-up shirt hugging his strong frame.

My fingers tingled with the need to reach out and touch his chest, be reminded of how good his muscles felt, how they hardened under my touch.

"Anything good?" he whispered, standing so close to me that I couldn't focus on anything but his breath on my face and his super sexy smell. When he reached over to the open book in my hands, his fingers grazed mine. A buzz shot up my hand and through my body. I shuddered in a way that made me putty around him.

I giggled and felt stupid because I needed to focus and not sound like Ava. Clearing my throat, I said, "Nothing here but snore fest material. You?"

"Dead end, but I learned some interesting, irrelevant

facts. Apparently in Turkey, Vampire derives from the word Upyr which means Witch. Oh, and in Romania to summon a Vampire all you need is a seven year old boy and a horse. This one baffles me. I get the boy being a meal, but what's with the horse?"

His words barely registered as his thumb stroked the back of my hand in circles and all I could focus on were his lips. Red and full, I wanted to kiss that mouth. When he caught me staring, I lowered my gaze, burning up from my head to toes.

His breathing quickened, his chest rising and falling quickly. His hand tightened against mine, and I looked up into rich mocha eyes filled with emotions that'd steal my breath, if had any left. All that stood between us was the book we held onto, barricading us.

With a free hand, he brushed a loose strand of hair caught in my lashes, his fingers gingerly caressing my cheek, coaxing shivers out of me. I stilled, frozen with fear and excitement.

Voices came from behind me and he pulled his hand away, breaking the perfect moment he'd created. Silence fell between us.

"Those Romanians Vamps are strange and believe in weird crap," I said, rambling. "When my cousins from there visited last, I caught their son in our background hypnotizing a small group of raccoons to do his bidding. He told me they were his freaking minions, can you believe it? For months after they left, we had those pesky animals trying to break into our house."

Was it suddenly really hot in here?

"Family can be strange."

His words reminded me of something from my last lesson. "Speaking of family, what did Mr. Leathers mean by the *infamous* Blackthorne Wolves?"

He raked his fingers through glossy curls of dark hair.

"He doesn't know what he's talking about. There's no infamy Mor. Not at all. Anyway, me and the guys have gotta go, we have a combat class to prepare for. Speak soon, yeah?" The corner of his mouth slid upward, and he brushed past me on purpose.

If I had a heart, it'd be skipping right now. I nodded and collapsed against the bookshelf, my gaze sliding to tight curve of Judas' ass as I chewed on my lower lip.

"You want him so bad." Ava's voice pierced the gaps in the books behind me.

I jerked my gaze toward her, my cheeks on fire. "Geez, want to scream it from the rooftop?"

She sauntered over, laughing to herself. "Mor, everyone already knows. They're just waiting for it to happen."

I glared at her. "For what to happen?"

"For you to kiss them already."

My mouth opened and then snapped shut.

Her blue eyes danced with excitement. "That's what I thought. Anyway, been thinking, let's hide the loot here at the Lodge so if anyone comes for them, they won't find them in your room. Maybe handing them to a teacher isn't such a smart idea. We don't know who sent them, or why. Once we figure that out, we can make a plan."

"You think someone will come for them?"

She shrugged and looped her arm around mine, tugging me into a walk. "Better to have them here than in your room, right?" She lifted a hand. "This is what we know; one, that Vamp vanished before he could say a damn word, which means he was being hunted; and two, we have no idea if these *are* actually diamonds, for all we know they could be a curse. Either way we shouldn't take the chance of someone coming for them."

"I'm bolting my doors and windows tonight."

Ava laughed and dragged me out of the library. "We can always have a slumber party."

"THE BOOK'S GOTTA be in here somewhere." Ava rummaged through the chest of drawers in her room.

I lay on my back across her bed, thoughts of diamonds and Judas' lips rushing through my mind. Soft lips, warm hands. What did a Wolf shifter taste like? He sure as hell smelled divine.

Ava slammed the drawer and huffed.

I lifted myself onto my elbows. "What are you looking for?"

She scratched her head. "Dad sent me this biography about the top clans in the country. Haven't read it, but maybe the Blackthorne pack is in there somewhere. Maybe pretty boy is hiding a deep, dark secret." She almost laughed, giddy with the idea of Judas having a juicy backstory.

"You don't need to enjoy yourself so much, do you?"

A malevolent chuckle slipped from her lips. "Bad boys are so much sexier you know."

"Is that why you're attracted to Chuck? You think he's a bad boy? Well, I've seen him fall asleep on the couch, snoring, and cuddling the family cat."

"Aww that's adorable," she cooed as she swooned across the room to the inbuilt wardrobe. "Speaking of Chuck, where is that big brute. I haven't seen him at all. A girl's starting to think he's avoiding her."

"A girl needs to get with the program, we're supposed to be hunting information about diamonds, not dark pasts and Vampire warriors." I rolled my eyes and collapsed back on the bed.

The diamonds were hidden in the pocket of my jacket draped over a chair at the Lodge. What if someone found them? But then again, what if they didn't...what then?

Ava strode across her room and yanked open her wardrobe. I caught the flare of pale fluff. There was a savage snarl before Ava squealed and slammed the door closed.

"What is it?" I shoved from the bed.

She was pale and shaking her head. "Nope, not going in there."

"What? What's in there?" Thoughts of Vampire creatures and severed heads rushed through my mind.

She turned before falling to her knees near the bed. She stuck her arm underneath then pulled out her wooden bat.

"What in the world are you doing?"

"The bunnies are gonna eat us while we sleep." She pointed to the wardrobe with her bat.

And now that we fell silent, I heard a faint, thump...thump...thump sound.

I took a step.

"Don't do it," she warned. "It can never be unseen."

I swallowed hard, gripped the handle and yanked.

The door flew open. Red eyes were all I saw...actually I *wish* they were all I saw.

The two demonic bunnies were...were...*wrestling,* my mind wanted to say, but they were doing a lot more than that. There, in between Ava's school shoes, were two bunnies fucking furiously like...rabbits. The one on top hissed, baring teeth at us, blood staining the fur around its mouth, and its partner was the same.

I slammed the door, screamed and stumbled backwards.

"I warned you," Ava muttered and gripped her bat.

A *thud* came from the wall between our rooms.

"Holy fuck, they're in the walls!" Ava stammered. "Put your stomping boots on," she declared, resting the bat over a shoulder, raising her chin. "We going bunny hunting."

"Says the girl who begged me to feed them demon blood."

"We were making a stand, protesting on behalf of the animals," she murmured. "Didn't think it'd turn out like this."

A tremble cut through my body. The corners of my mouth twitched.

Ava turned toward me, caught the smile as it stretched my lips.

A snigger broke free, and in an instant, we were laughing so hard there were tears in her eyes. Ava lifted a hand and pointed to the cupboard. "I am *not* wearing those sneakers *ever again.*"

Her words only made my knees shudder as I collapsed onto the bed.

"Did you see where they were biting?" Ava howled. "Makes new meaning to the term *angry sex.*"

"*Oh!*" I roared and held my stomach. "Oh my God."

"Kinda kinky if you think about it," she added.

"*Ava!*" I wailed and reached over, slapping her arm.

We laughed so hard we drowned out the sounds in that cupboard.

"We're so fucked." Ava cried and laughed.

"No, they are!" I followed and buried my head into the comforter. We snorted and giggled, and flinched every now and then when a *thud* came from the walls. Ava gripped the baseball bat and we lay there until the ache in our bellies eased and we could breathe.

"Let's go." She giggled. "Maybe we can find more along the footpath."

"God, can you imagine Ms. Lucas finding them?" I sniggered. "She'd pitch a damn fit."

"Serves her right," Ava snarled and pushed from the bed.

We made our way out of the room, down the stairs and out of the dorm. The sky was darkening, and stars sparkled. My thoughts turned to the diamonds. I glanced along the walkway as we turned left and took the path around the back of the main building.

A rabbit squealed, hissed and tore across the footpath in front of us, heading close to the dark pond. In an instant, a huge gold colored fish leaped out of the water, snatched the rabbit mid-air and hit the ground with a *slap*. Fins twitched and flapped furiously. The fish was like nothing I'd seen before. It squirmed and writhed, working its way back toward the water as we stopped and stared.

Until its tail slipped under the surface of the water and both fish and rabbit disappeared under a flurry of bubbles and splashes.

"What the fuck was that." I jerked my gaze to Ava.

She just stared at the place where the thing had been, her cheeks flushed, eyes wide. But it was more than shock...it was *haunting*.

"There's monster fish in the river?" I muttered. "A *golden* monster fish."

Ava erupted into a nervous laughter and stumbled toward me, shoving her hand against the small of my back and pushed. "That was something, wow. Let's maybe head back." She glanced over her shoulder at the river as she walked away.

"What aren't you telling me?" I twisted, trying to catch her gaze.

"It's a long story," she muttered. "I'll tell you one day."

She refused to look at me, but I wasn't a fool.

One way or another, I'd find out what the hell that golden fish was in the pond, and why it felt like all my damn friends were keeping secrets.

CHAPTER SEVEN

ORGASMS AND DIAMONDS. A VAMP'S BEST FRIEND

We ate in silence. Once more Judas and the Wolves were gone. I sat back and watched Ava devour two steamed fish, and then curl her nose at the salad. "You want this?" She pushed the greens toward me.

I just raised a brow and looked at her as she muttered under her breath and dragged the plate close once more.

"They're not here," she murmured, drawing my gaze to the table.

"I know that."

"So why the tension? This whole Blackthorne pack has you riled up."

I lifted my gaze to hers. She was right. "Don't you think I should be worried? I mean, why would Nefarious say something like that in the first place, if he didn't want me to know what the deal was. And why does Judas evade the question if it really is nothing. Why not tell me and get it all out in the open?"

She shoved a mass of green leaves around her plate. "Either there's something to hide or there isn't, but in bringing it up in the first place he's forcing you to pick sides."

And then there were the diamonds.... "Maybe we should grab my *jacket* from the library."

It was Ava's turn to cock her head. The *'code'* earned me a snarl. "We made a plan, you need to stick to it."

I sighed and leaned backwards, listening to the chatter and the drone all around me. She was right. I knew she was right, and still there was something inside me that made my stomach clench with fear.

Transcendence. The word slipped in amongst the worry. I glanced at the mess on her place and rose. "You ready?"

"You're not eating?" she asked for the third time.

My stomach churned as I shook my head. "I'm heading back. You take your time."

She just nodded, letting me turn and walk away. I headed along the hall, this time passing my Ancient Studies classroom. The light was on inside, blazing like a damn invitation. I slowed and then stopped outside the door.

My knuckles barely made a sound on the wooden surface. So I sighed and then rapped my knuckles on the door again.

There was no answer, so I turned the handle and stepped into the enclave before the room. "Mr. Leathers?"

Silence greeted me; maybe he was gone.

There was a scuff in a walkway on the other side of the classroom. A grunt followed, then a growl, low, sinister...warning.

"Nefarious?" I called out a little louder.

Fear danced along my spine as that growl turned into words. "Come between us again, and there won't be a body left to find."

I stopped in the middle of the classroom and stared into

the darkened hallway. Silver eyes glinted in the dark. I knew those eyes and *that* voice.

Judas had hold of Nefarious Leathers. One strong forearm was across his chest, driving him hard against the wall of the walkway. Hate mingled with rage. Wolf against Vampire. Both men glared at each other. Only Nefarious curled his lips into a smile and murmured. "Woops. Looks like your girlfriend knows what kind of boyfriend you really are."

Judas gave him a shove and then stepped away, never once taking his eyes off my teacher. "That's the only warning you're going to get."

I wanted to meet those silver eyes as Judas turned and glared at the ground, but everything about him made me want to turn and run.

He lifted his head as he strode out of the walkway and into the classroom. Pain savaged his beautiful brown eyes as they found mine.

I wanted to run to him, wanted to wrap my arms around him and never let go. I wanted to hold him, and comfort him as he'd comforted me. I took a slow step until he curled his lips. "He's right. Don't, Mor. Don't come near me."

He cut across the other side of the teacher's table, shoving the chair as he strode toward the door. The loud *bang* shuddered the glass inside the door frame. I flinched at the sound and then turned to Mr. Leathers as he tugged down his shirt.

"What the hell was all that about?"

White fangs peeked out from under the Vampire's lips as he muttered. "Seems Mr. Blackthorne didn't like being outed."

Anger flared as he stepped into the light. "So why the hell did you do it in the first place?"

"Because." He met my gaze and stepped closer. "I thought it was time you knew what you were getting into."

It was my dad all over again. The sneering. The warning. The pretending they knew better.

I just met his stare with my own. "I guess time will tell then, won't it *Mr. Leathers.*" Before I turned and strode away.

I hurried through the classroom and the out of the door. But Judas was nowhere to be seen. Maybe I could catch him on the walkway. I smiled at the others milling around in the hallway, watching me as I raced past.

Everyone treated me differently now. My mom, Dad, even Chuck to a degree. It's like I'd turned one hundred and sprouted another damn head. I was still the same Vampire. Still the same daughter, still the same student.

"Ms. Livingstone," Principal Stone snapped as I rushed past.

I ignored whatever she said next, pushing open the door before I raced out into the right. A darkened blur caught my eye as I hurried along the footpath. I caught sight of Judas as he ran. *"Judas wait!"*

He slowed, and then stopped, before he turned toward me. He looked dark and mysterious, glossy curls shining under the silver moon. Every bit a Wolf to be careful of. But I wasn't careful where he was concerned.

I wasn't careful at all.

He sucked in hard breaths, eyes pleading before he shook his head and then turned once more. He left me then, disappearing between the pine trees.

"What the Hell," I murmured.

I could've raced after him. I could've caught him if I wanted to.

But he didn't want me too. That was evident.

Instead I made my way back to the dorm, yanked open the door and climbed the stairs to my room.

"Everyone's scared of you, Vampire."

I stilled at the top of the stairs and turned to the shadows. Nesrin took a step. Black hair shimmering almost blue under the overhead lights.

"They're scared of what they don't know."

We were once enemies. Her and her Cat gang had stolen my spelled ring and left me to die in an abandoned church at the edge of the academy grounds, that was until Ava and the Wolves found me.

They'd stayed with me, protected me...they'd fought for me.

"Are you scared of me." I took a step toward her.

"More, silently cautious," she answered, her green eyes flaring to life.

"Good," I murmured. "You should be."

And then I turned and headed for my room, leaving her standing there half hidden in the dark. I had nothing more to say to Nesrin nothing that would bring her the kind of peace she was seeking.

The light was on under Ava's door. A shadow cut across her room before her bed springs gave that familiar *twang*. Most nights we hung out together, talking, laughing...hiding bodies in the basement. But tonight, I wanted to be alone with the books...and my thoughts.

I slipped inside and closed the door behind me before hitting the bedside light. And in that moment between darkness and light my stomach tightened and I caught my breath. The yellow hue brightened, casting shadows into the corners...it was the exact same as I left it.

I strode over to the balcony. There were no small Vampire creatures waiting for me. No weird packages left on my floor. There weren't even clothes scattered anymore. Everything was neat and clean. Everything was just as it should be. I strode into the bathroom, turned on the light and hit the lever for the shower.

Steam rose after a second, filling the space as I undressed and then stepped into the spray, washing and then rinsing, letting the water sluice the cold away. But I couldn't shake the pain in Judas' gaze, or Mr.. Leather's warning away. I hit the tap and stepped out, hurried to dry, and climbed between my sheets.

The heavy book Nefarious gave me still sat on the end of the bed. The thing was big enough to make the corner of the mattress dip. I yanked it closer and opened to the table of contents.

Transcendence Vampire. My fingers raced along the list of words. But there was nothing. *Vampire - Divine Being, Transcend.* I stilled, traced my finger along the page number and then flicked through the pages until I found it.

There was the image of a Vampire, long fangs, pale silver skin. He had his hands placed together, palms facing upwards and in the middle of his hold were two white doves.

The Transcendic Vampire uses Divine Traits to become more than an Immortal Creature.

I pulled the book closer...*ascendance to true Godhood.* "True Godhood? What the hell does that even mean?" I kept reading, taking in every bit of information I could find. It wasn't much, but it was enough to fill me with dread. I shook my head and pushed the book away. "He's got it wrong. That's not me. That's not me at all."

I settled down against the pillows. "Godhood my ass."

The idea plagued me though, digging in like thorny tendrils and wrapping around my thoughts. Exhaustion followed and I closed my eyes. The bedside light was bright against my lids, but I was weighed down by the day...unable to lift my arms, or surface long enough to switch it off.

*"B*LACKTHORNE *W*OLVES ARE DANGEROUS, *M*ORWENNA*." I turned to see Nefarious Leathers cutting across the classroom toward me. "I'm only telling you for your own good. Wolves don't belong with Vampires...Vampires belong with Vampires."*

I shook my head, taking a step backwards. "I don't think so..."

Perfect lips curled into a smile as my teacher came closer and lifted his hand, fingers brushing a strand of hair from the side of my face. "I do."

I swallowed hard, trying my best to tear my gaze from the sleeveless shirt and the hard muscles underneath. "I'm pretty sure there's a law against this, right?"

"Against what...a teacher and a student?"

His finger trailed to the edge of my chin and then lifted until I met this gaze.

This was wrong. This wasn't what I wanted.

"We could be powerful together," Nefarious murmured and lowered his head.

I closed my eyes, inhaling deep, and with the musty classroom air, I drew the taste of him.

Cold lips brushed against mine. His fingers never trembled, or even moved.

He knew what he was doing, from the crush of his lips, to the slow trail of the back of his finger down the length of my neck.

And his lips followed, leaving mine as he bent his neck. I craned my head to the side, letting him go where he wanted.

Sure hands skimmed the outside of my body and reached around to cup the curve of my ass.

"I'm going to taste you, Morwenna... I'm going to taste you and lick you and take you places no Wolf can. You will transcend laying under me...you will touch God."

If I had a heart it would hammer, and I'd breathe so fast I couldn't catch it.

I shook my head, tearing away from his hold. "No. I don't want that...I don't want you."

And as desire flooded through me and welled between my thighs...he whispered. "Oh, I think you do."

I jerked my eyes open as my body pulsed between my thighs. I shoved a hand between my legs and clamped down. But it was too late. My orgasm hit me, wave after blinding wave. I turned my head and buried my face into my pillow as a cry tore free and I heard the *clink, click, clink* of something familiar. I opened my eyes and stared at the purple bag next to my pillow... I didn't need to look inside to know what they were. The diamonds were back, and they brought with them erotic dreams of my goddamn teacher.

*I don't want that...*my own words echoed.

But the answer filled me as my body shuddered one last time and fell still...*Oh...I think you do.*

CHAPTER EIGHT

DREAMS TURNED TO NIGHTMARES

"Hey!" Ava called out behind me. "Wait the hell up."

But I never slowed, only lengthened my stride and clenched my grip around the book in my arms.

"What the Hell's gotten into you?" Ava huffed scurrying to keep up with me.

I ground my jaw and tried to keep from answering her. 'cause she wouldn't like the answer…oh no she wouldn't. So, I stayed quiet, saying nothing as I headed for the east building.

The bell rang overhead, loud and shrill. It'd make me flinch if I wasn't already pissed.

I reached out, gripped the handle of the front door and yanked. The handle slammed against the stone wall with a *bang* before I strode through. Students stopped dead in the middle of the hallway, stopped and then turned, watching me as I strode past and made for the classroom.

I yanked the handle, sucked in a hard breath and steeled my nerve.

Ava stood, watching me as I strode inside.

Nefarious lifted his head with a look of surprise as I strode in. "Morwenna...I wasn't expecting you until—"

"Take your damn book." I heaved the thick textbook from my hands and dropped it to his desk with a *boom!* And then leaned over the desk to stab him in the chest. "And stay the Hell out of my dreams, *Mr. Leathers.*"

He flinched, glanced to the book and then back to me before he gave a shake of his head. "I don't—"

"—Oh, I think you do," I lowered my gaze...and kicked myself. *Why did you do that? Why did you look at him?* And in my head all I could feel was his fingers sliding down the vein in my neck. "You..." I jerked my gaze to his. "You just stay the hell out of my dreams."

He stiffened, one brow rising.

So, help me, if you smile...

There was a twitch at the corner of his lips, but no smile...not yet, as he murmured. "Dreams, Ms. Livingstone? What kind of dreams?"

My cheeks burned. "That's none of your business."

But he just turned and glanced at the book on his desk. "If the book is speaking to you, then it could very well be important."

"Oh, I doubt it's the book that's whispering in my ear, Mr. Leathers. I doubt that very much."

"Oh?" he murmured. "And are you an expert on dreamology?"

I closed my mouth.

"I didn't think so," he answered. "I, on the other hand, have done extensive research into the subliminal messages our brains create into fantasy. Please." He motioned at the seat next to his desk. "Talk to me, maybe together we can figure this out."

I glanced to the door and the hallway. Ava was probably still waiting for me...or then again, maybe she wasn't.

The diamonds.

I slipped my hand into my pocket. *Clink...clink...*my fingers skimmed soft felt before the material warmed under my hand. *Tell him...*the words echoed through my mind. I swallowed hard as heat filled me, pulsing between my legs and licking my nipples. "I...*ah*...I had a dream where you...."

"Yes," he murmured and rose to stand. My body tightened, breath came at a rush. I hated how I wanted him...hated how I felt.

"You—"

A scream swallowed the word, piercing, unmerciful...filled with rage. My heart lunged as I jerked my head toward the doorway. I was already moving before I realized, striding toward the doorway.

"Wait, Morwenna," Nefarious called as I reached for the handle.

But I was backed into a corner by seductive dreams and all the things good girls didn't do. But I wasn't a good girl. I was Morwenna Livingstone. I twisted the handle and stepped out into the chaos. Nesrin jerked her gaze toward me from the other side of the hallway. Her chest rose in hard breaths, lips parted, eyes wide. There was a smear of blood on her cheek as she lifted her head.

And from the corner of my eye I caught two black-eyed demon students lunge with bloodied hands raised in the air.

"They killed our teacher," Nesrin gasped across the space as a rush of students tore past. "Ripped his goddamn head clean off."

I flinched as more frantic students screamed clamored, clawing the people next to them to get toward the front door of the building.

Sunlight flooded the space, glinting in my eyes as two towering shadows stepped into the doorway and pushed through the frantic fray. One towered over the other students, all brawn and thick muscles. I didn't need to see their faces to know who they were.

My dad strode toward me, holding a cage in his hand, and behind him, the towering Vampire warrior, Chuck.

"Mor!" Ava screamed in the distance.

I jerked my gaze toward her, and stepped out of the doorway. A young female Vamp shouldered me backwards as she rushed past. Her eyes widened, registering in an instant who I was. But then she was gone, stumbling away from the terror.

Behind her a Demon lunged across the hallway and hit a male student head on. He gripped his shoulders and bit his neck, savaging and tearing. Blood sprayed into the air, splashing the walls and the floor. Other students slipped in the mess, scurrying to their feet as they ran.

"Morwenna," Dad called not bothering with the horror one bit as he lifted the metal carrier and snarled. "This...*thing* is yours."

Tiny claws speared through the gaps of the cage in his hand. Underneath the horrendous sounds of terror, I could hear the hiss and snarl of the honey badger, Dad's birthday gift to me....

"Dad," I muttered as a guttural snarl rippled through the hallway. "I don't think now's the time."

"This is *exactly* the right time," he answered coldly.

A sickening, guttural snarl rumbled from behind me. I turned, finding myself face to face with the murderous gaze of a Demon. Midnight-eyes shone under the overhead lights, making his pale skin even more washed out. He was just one of us, blond hair, long nails, dressed in his Bestias Academy uniform. But his teeth were coated with blood, and chunks of skin and veins dripped from his mouth as he snarled and then turned his head.

But there was something in the way he looked at me, and then his gaze dropped to the pocket of my jacket...like somehow he just *knew*.

He knew what was in there.

He *knew* what the diamonds were.

The Demon smiled, lifted his gaze from my pocket to my face, then opened his mouth, and with a sinister snarl he lunged. Chuck moved faster than a man his size should, striding forward as he reached for his waist and drew out a black tipped steel dagger.

I stumbled backwards, my heart driving into my throat as the *squelch* of the blow filled the air and Chuck stabbed the Demon in the heart.

Dad never moved, only watched...like he'd seen it all a hundred times before. The Demon stumbled backwards and dropped his gaze to his chest. "I...I didn't mean."

"It's done now," Chuck murmured, gripping him by the shoulder and ramming the blade deep.

But as the Demon in his hands curled his lips and shoved to stand, another Demon stepped out of the classroom in front of Ava, took one look at the dying immortal in Chuck's hands and then lunged.

There was no way Chuck could protect me and also save himself.

But there was no way he'd ever see me harmed.

And so, he moved, striding out to take the full brunt of the attack.

Thick, squelching arms lashed out of Ava as the Demon

went for the Vampire warrior. In a second her beast filled the hallway, all blood-red suckers and pale shimmering skin. Red markings flared against her jawline and ran along her cheek. She was magnificent and terrifying all at once, and if I hadn't seen her beast before I would've fainted.

Red lips were the same burgundy blood-red as the curved marks that ran underneath her shirt. She was stronger, and faster, more terrifying than ever before...and as I turned to the Vampire warrior standing in front of me...I saw Chuck go perfectly still.

He stared as she dragged the Demon into her, devouring every bone and terrifying cell of the Demon. He dropped the dead body in his grasp, and gripped the hilt of the dagger tight as his lips parted...and Ava severed and swallowed...until there was nothing left.

And in a slow, hollow thud of my heart the Great Creature of the Sea was gone.

And my best friend was there once more, so small...so pale, stumbling sideways as I rushed toward her.

"Did I save him?" she croaked as her knees buckled. "Is Chuck...okay?"

"I'm here," the deep growl of the warrior came behind me.

He bowed his head toward me, and then slipped his hands under mine. "I have her," he growled.

And I knew that he did.

I slid my hands out from underneath her, and the warrior took my place as the door to the classroom opened behind me.

Nefarious Leathers glanced along the corridor and stepped out.

"I came to see..." he started and then turned his head

and met my father's gaze. "Oh, my word...Dante Living-stone as I live and not breathe."

I flinched, waiting for the spray of Vampire blood.

No one called my father by his first name.

Not if they wanted to live.

CHAPTER NINE

TO HELL AND BACK IN A HANDBASKET

"Oh, flagellation of the wicked, what in the Ancient's name is going on here?" Dad seethed at Mr. Leathers, before marching down the hallway.

The tails of his coat flapped behind him, slapping together like cracks of a whip and for those few moments, he embodied the clichéd epitome of a Vampire, tall, dark, and very...*very*...deadly.

I winced and scurried after him.

"*Dad!* Dad, stop," I called as he marched.

But he never slowed, not for anyone. Students and teachers jumped out of his path, and pressed their spine against their lockers. I didn't know who they feared more; murderous Demons or my Dad—probably Dad—if they were smart.

He shoved open the door at the end of the corridor and vanished outside into the day.

"Hell, he looks ready to murder someone." Ava sidled up to my side, staring at the door flapping shut.

"Yep, my life's about to be hell in a handbasket." My nerves were on edge, and I had to fix this now. "Gotta go." I took off, running after him. Outside, I swung left, scanning the grounds until I spied him turning the corner toward the front of the main building.

Shit!

I darted forward, picturing him causing chaos in the office, throwing out threats like hand grenades. Bursting in through the front doors, I swung right toward the Principal's office, but Dad's snarling voice caught my attention from the left. I pivoted on my heels and rushed into a waiting room with an enormous fireplace and two walls covered in bookshelves.

Principal Stone stood deathly still, staring Dad in the eyes, not backing down. Brave woman.

Daddy Dearest shouted in her face, "This wasn't our agreement. If it wasn't for the Ancient...." They both stared at me standing in the open archway to the room.

Dad pointed at me, his face darkening. "Demons attacked her on school grounds in broad daylight!"

Ms. Stone swallowed loudly and squared her shoulders, her jawline tight. "This has never happened in our school before." She turned to me, glaring.

"You're saying my daughter caused this?" He seemed to grow in size. "You promised me safety."

Principal Stone snapped back toward my dad. "Mr. Livingstone, our campus grounds are spelled weekly—"

"I'm tired of lame excuses. Maybe I need to have more of my guards positioned here. You *obviously* can't ensure your students' safety. But *I* sure as damn Hell can."

My mouth opened with a protest as I moved into the room, but Ms. Stone's lips curled into a snarl.

I knew what Dad's version of safety was. I'd be back behind bullet proof glass, hidden in a vault just like our home. That's not what I wanted...not now, not when I was finally...*finding myself.*

"That is not necessary." The Principal held his gaze with her own. "This will *never* happen again, I give you my word."

"That means nothing to me when it comes to Morwenna's wellbeing."

I stuffed my hand into my pocket, my fingers coiled around velvety bag, and the emblem that no longer sent electricity surging through my fingers.

"I think I know what the demons wanted," I said in between the screaming match.

They both snapped around toward me, the fury on their faces quickly replaced with curiosity. Dad's titled his head, eyeing me sharply

"Well, speak up."

I pulled the bag out of my pocket and placed it in his hands. "A small hunchback Vampire with glowing eyes came to my room a few nights ago, saying he needed help, then he left these in my room."

"You let him into your room?" Principal Stone's voice climbed.

"Morwenna," Dad snapped, pulling open the ties on the bag. "I taught you better than that."

"Well, he said he needed help. I thought maybe someone was chasing him." I fidgeted with the hem of my school shirt. "Anyway, Dad, you told me to always help someone in need."

His head flinched upward, disbelief washing over his expression. Oh, right, that might have been Mom saying that.

The cords in his muscles tensed, and he turned toward the principal. "Why was a sewer dweller breaking into your campus! Thought you said you had the place locked down?"

Ms. Stone was breathing faster than a normal person should. "We have, I mean I will check this week's spell was done."

Dad grumbled under his breath.

"What's a sewer dweller?" I asked, but they ignored me, both of their gazes falling to the sparkly stones rolling out of the bag and into Dad's large palm.

The principal gasped, her hand flying to her chest in an exaggerated gesture. Had she never seen a diamond before? Instinct had me glancing at her fingers. No rings.

Dad grabbed my wrist, studying my palm, then my other hand, stopping on the index finger that got zapped when I touched the emblem on the bag the other day.

His brow furrowed into a tangled mess. "They've marked her," he growled.

"Marked," I breathed and pulled my hand back before staring and prodding the red tip of my finger that had never completely healed.

"Have you tried to get rid of them?" He snapped toward me.

I nodded, twisting the family ring around my middle finger, the one that allowed me to walk in daylight, but didn't protect me against whatever these diamonds were. I told Dad about hiding the stones and how they returned to my room. Maybe I was stuck in a damn Groundhog day with them.

Dad reached over and cupped my cheek. "The diamonds have been marked by your power, and your power has marked them."

"What the hell does that mean? How do I unmark myself?" I failed to hide the tremble in my voice.

"Whoever's marked you and the diamonds now has access to your power. I've heard of these stones before. It won't drain you but they could make you too strong."

Why was that a bad thing?

"It could destroy you, Morwenna."

Before I could respond, Dad dragged me into his arms, constricting me against his chest. "This was why I didn't want you to leave home or go to an Academy." Trepidation lined his whispered words. "Hell, damn the Reckoning of the Dead. Nothing good in having you attend here."

I wriggled free from his iron embrace and glanced up, noting Ms. Stone was walking out of the room, Dad's gaze followed her and it was clear his conversation with her wasn't finished.

"What do I do now?" I asked.

He kissed the top of my head. "Go to class. Leave it to me." With a quick nod he marched after the Principal and into her office, closing the door behind him.

I stood there, feeling like ice flooded my veins. Who the hell would want my power when I couldn't even master it myself? Then I recalled Mr. Leathers' statement about me being the most powerful Vampire. He had to be mistaken.

And I wasn't going to sit around. Dad had given me a clue, and I intended to do my own investigation into who in the world had targeted me, and how to remove the damn mark.

"Sewer dweller?" Judas wiped his mouth with a paper napkin and cast it into the middle of a now empty plate.

The cafeteria crowd was starting to thin, leaving a few of us behind.

I stared at Judas from across the table. "So, you up for an exploration mission with me?"

The words felt forced. I hated that. But I hated the way Leathers had come between us even more, so this was my damn olive branch.

All he had to do was take it.

When he didn't answer, I reached over and touched his arm, turning around in my seat to face him. "Is everything all right?"

It took him a moment to respond and when he did, it wore a forced smile. "Yeah, just a few things on my mind. Is it okay if I ask Nero to tag along instead?"

"*Nero?* Sure."

"Bond's busy. I've got...pack stuff. But Nero's a solid guy. He'll keep you safe."

He glanced toward the doorway, his voice trailing away. He was occupied by something...and that something wasn't me. He grabbed his tray from the table and rose from the seat. "I'll catch you later, okay?"

"Okay," I murmured watching as he stood from the table and then strode away.

The foul sound of sniggering cut across the space. I wrenched my head toward the sound and glared at Nesrin. *Bitch.*

She fucking riled me, worming her way under my skin, like she had done since the day I arrived here. I shoved from the seat and turned, and collided right into Nero, whose arms snapped around my waist to stop me from tripping backward.

"Whoa, I got you." He murmured.

My hands went to his chest and I fell into his deep blue eyes. He had the thickest, longest eyelashes, and coupled with his raven hair and tanned skin, I suddenly forgot about everything else. His fingers dug into my back with urgency, and I hitched an invisible breath all the way down to my lungs.

"So, I hear I'm escorting you on a search mission," he stated in a smooth, deep voice that left me tingling.

A smile crept over his mouth, and the air around us seemed thicker, heavier.

"You heard that huh?" I murmured, trying not to get lost in his eyes.

"You'd be amazed at what I hear," He murmured. "So, where are we going?"

I chewed my bottom lip and tried to think. "I have no idea at this point."

"Geez, get a room you two. And you can do better, Nero," Nesrin snarled as she passed, and the anger in her eyes showed jealousy. Her feline followers made gagging sounds.

I stepped away from Nero, but he never took his eyes off me, instead he trailed fingers down my arm and grasped my hand.

Butterflies fluttered in my chest at the touch.

Heck, there was a whole zoo in there running rampant.

Was I really attracted to three guys at once?

And they encouraged it.

"I think Nesrin has a crush on you," I teased, lost in my own moment, loving how incredible it felt to be walking hand in hand with him.

But he never looked at her, even now when her name was on his lips. "We dated once."

I tried to swallow my flinch. "Really?"

He shrugged as if the news meant nothing. "Last year she pounced on me on my first day at the Academy. After two weeks, she dumped me for Bond, then went to Judas, trying to turn us against one another. Didn't work though. She didn't understand the rules. The pack shares everything."

Was it wrong of me to be happy none of the Wolves were interested in Nesrin? Even if I couldn't stop the smile from creeping across my lips.

"What's the plan?" Nero asked. "Dad always says never wander aimlessly, always have a plan."

I shook my head, and the sting from Nesrin's spiteful sniggers fading. "All I know is we need to find a sewer dweller. That's what dad called it."

"Sewer...the ones that run under the city," he was lost in his thoughts, blue eyes sparkling like the clearest ocean. "There's lots of manholes in the streets. I know of a few that could lead us down to where we need to go."

I shuddered at the thought of doing *down there*. But answers waited in the darkness, answers I needed.

"The city," I murmured.

His smile was fast, "Nice day for a jog?"

I stared at him, the life draining from my face. "You've got to be kidding, right?"

A bark of laughter followed as he took a step backwards and threw open his hands. "What, you don't want to get shown up by a Wolf, Vampire?"

I ground my jaw. "Like Hell." And then strode forward.

There was no way some...gorgeous, blue-eyed furball was going to outpace a Livingstone.

No helldamned way.

I followed him out of the cafeteria and then the building before we cut across the parking lot and headed for the trees. Twigs snapped and crunched under my feet. His laughter flew back into my face as he took off across the ground.

I lunged after him. Trees whipped past at a blur, and I became the hunter once more and as we left the Academy grounds behind and headed for the towering skyscrapers of the city the game consumed me.

I caught sight of him racing ahead before he pivoted on a dime and leapt over a fallen tree. But I was on his tail, charging until my hair whipped behind me and my skirt plastered against my thighs, and finally we tore out of the trees and into an open field.

Nero slowed down, letting me catch him and together we slipped and raced along footpaths, eventually leaving the open ground behind.

Cars whipped past us, some we paced, rushing to surge ahead only to turn at the last moment and slip down a side street.

"Not far," Nero lifted his hand. "Two, maybe three blocks."

He reached out, grasped my hand and slowed our pace. I let him lead the way, sucking in hard breaths as I relished the feel of his warm hand around mine. It was nice to be cared about for something more than just designer clothes and limousines.

The city traffic slowed the deeper into the city we went, cars crawled bumper to bumper as we ran from building to building, turning down darkened side-streets and wove our way to some place Nero knew of.

"There" he jerked his head toward an empty street. "See that covered manhole? That's going to get us where we need to be."

He slowed, sucking in hard breaths, his cheeks bright red from the run, and glanced behind us. The side-street was empty, cars lined each side, most of the buildings were apartment complexes, with a few small boutique stores toward the main street.

Nero dropped my hand, bent and worked his fingers into the small hollow before he heaved. Muscles strained, flexing under his shirt, and with a scrape, the heavy covering came free.

"Careful going down," he peered into the dark. "Looks like the ladder doesn't go all the way to the bottom.

I stepped closer, and then crouched, my skirt fluttering with the movement. Not the best clothing for drafts of wind, but it was too damn late to change now.

I reached down, pressed the hemline to my thighs and stole a breath. "Okay, here goes nothing."

My shoe sank into the darkness as I lowered my foot through the hole and found the first rung. One after another I stepped down, grasping rusted metal as I went.

Nero was right. My foot searched for another rung, but found only air. I looked down, finding nothing but air and stared at the ground far below. I clenched my jaw, muttered a *oh shit,* and then let go.

I hit the ground with a *thud.* The sudden jolt tearing through my ankles and raced along my legs. But I made it. I made it and...*eww...gross...*the place was *rank.*

Nero landed beside me and screwed his nose at the disgusting smell. "Rubbish. God humans are gross." He reached out and grasped my hand. "Come on, when we get to the storm water it'll pass."

I let him lead me, along darkened tunnels filled with rodents and piles of trash and eventually the smell left.

"Does everyone know about these tunnels?"

He shrugged. "Those in the know."

I pulled out the small flashlight in my pocket and switched

it on, a bright orange beam lighting the way, bouncing over the brick walls. Without another word, we kept moving deeper and deeper. When we reached a fork in the path, Nero nudged right... of course, because it was darker and rank.

The passage slowly descended and the smell worsened, water splashed underfoot, and I didn't want to know what we waded through.

Who knew how long we'd walked for, all we'd seen were brick walls, no signs of life or a sewer dweller. Maybe I'd been wrong to assume it would be that easy.

"What's that?" Nero pointed at something ahead, and I froze, fear zipping up my spine.

When I waved the light about, the beam landed on pentacle marking on the wall. But what was that? I squinted. From our angle I could swear there was someone slumped on the ground, and a chill rushed up my spine.

We hurried closer, water splashing under our fast foot-steps, my gaze locked on the figure. Whoever it was lay on their side, mostly covered by a cape, their head pointed in the opposite direction.

Nero's breath sped at seeing the victim. Once we reached the figure, Nero leaned over the body, pulling back the hood.

I peered over Nero's shoulder, iciness clawing into my chest as I stared down into a familiar face. It was the hunch-back Vampire. He lay lifeless, blue faced, and smelling. How long had he been down here?

"Oh, shit! That's him, the Vamp who came to my room in the middle of the night."

"Looks like he's dead, dead. Not Vampire dead." He glanced over at me.

"I know what dead means." But I couldn't stop staring

at the body, while Nero checked his body for any marks or injuries.

I wrapped my arms around my middle. Someone followed him all the way down here.

Someone who came here with one purpose.

And it looked like that purpose was to kill.

CHAPTER TEN

REJECTION TASTES LIKE DIRT!

"It's not right." Nero stared at the markings on the wall above the Vamp's body and stepped closer. "See that, the corner doesn't touch the circle there."

"So? There's a dead Vampire!" I squinted. How in the Hell can he see that, anyway? Must be a Wolf thing.

"What do you mean, 'so?'" He cut me a glare, but then smiled. "You really don't understand magic at all, do you?"

I shook my head, but it seemed he did.

"If the corners don't touch then there's no spell. You need the power of all four; north, south, east, and west to call anything. It's like Witching 101."

I took a step toward the body of the creature and knelt beside him. "Well, whatever it was...it must have killed him, and it looks like a Witches mark to me."

He turned his head, looking at something on the ground, and sniffed the air.

"What is it?"

His boots scuffed in the dim light as Nero strode across the tunnel and kneeled. He skimmed his finger across something on the ground, and then lifted it to his nose and inhaled. "Blood, Demon Blood."

There was a shake of his head as I shoved upwards. "I don't think this was done by a Witch. I'll prove it to you, but the most important question is what *did* kill him." He headed for the body once more, swiping fingers on his jeans before he opened the creatures shirt, exposing pale skin and a skeletal body underneath.

"There's no mark," he murmured. "Not that I can see. I'm betting that we could search the Vampire from top to bottom and still not find a thing. Someone wants to us to believe this was done by a Witch, but this just feels too...*sloppy,* not like them at all."

"How do you know?"

He turned his gaze toward me, blue eyes shone, even in the dark. "You trust me, right?" He came closer. "I want you to meet someone. Someone who'll tell you straight up if Witches are involved one way or another."

"Okay," I murmured. "But first I need to message Chuck."

I reached into my pocket and yanked my phone free. My fingers flew across the screen.

Mor: Dead Vamp Body in tunnels under the city. 245th Street. Take manhole in middle of street, watch out for rats.

I shoved my phone back into my pocket before taking Nero's hand. We could be like any other couple, kicking rusted cans and scurrying rats out of the way as we made our way back to where the tunnel rose.

The sewer snaked around the part of the city, until it joined the storm drains with a deafening roar. Droplets of water splattered my cheek until Nero turned, gripped my waist and then heaved me into the air. I clutched the sides of the ladder, hooking a foot against the metal rung and then climbed, looking over my shoulder to see him hunker down and then lunge. Wolves sure made light work of being agile, and strong...and gorgeous for that matter.

It was lucky Nero was with me...

He'd always been quieter than the other two, leaving his eyes to say all he needed to say. I'd caught him staring at me when he thought I wasn't looking, and even though Judas had been the one to carry me from that abandoned church when I was hurt, both Bond and Nero were there, forging through beside us, making sure Judas raced me inside.

They were also the ones who got my ring back from the cat gang. For that I'd owe them my life. I reached overhead and shoved the iron grate against the street.

"Careful," Nero murmured.

His hand skimmed my calf, and then my thigh, pushing the hemline of my skirt higher. His breath warm against my skin as he climbed, pressing me against the metal rows.

The juncture of his hips met the curve of my thigh. I stilled, closed my eyes and clamped my legs tight as my heart gave a pathetic *thud,* and heat followed, licking between my thighs.

Dear God, this was so not happening.

"Gotta be careful," he murmured in my ear as he reached up, gripped the rim of the opening and then heaved his powerful frame upwards.

He made it seem so fucking easy, climbing through the hole to stand in the middle of the street overhead.

He smiled down at me, crouched and offered his hand. "Don't want you to lose your head."

Those words should *not* have been sexy. Nor should traipsing through muddied sewer water with rats and Hell knew what all around us.

But it was sexy, so help me to Hell and back, it was. I

just smiled, swallowed hard and took his hand. He heaved me up through the hole and then slid the grate home.

He chuckled and shook his head.

"What?" I brushed cobwebs and dirt from my skirt, and eyed him.

"You acted like I asked for your hand in marriage." He glanced at the cars tearing past us and then found my gaze. "You don't have to be so guarded around me you know. I'd never do anything you didn't want."

My breath caught. I forced a smile. "I know that."

But inside I was jumpy and nervous, watching him from the corner of my eye as he scanned the traffic and grabbed my hand once more. "Let's go. It's not too far from here."

My hair flew back as we ran to the other side of the street and then along the footpath. I had no idea where we were going, nor did I care. Nero turned and smiled at me, setting the pace with long, sure strides.

Shops and grocery stores blurred together. We ran until we passed one mortal police station and then another, lunging from the pavement to the street to the pavement again.

I knew the city, well I thought I did. But as we turned one corner and slipped down an alley we came out to a part of the city I'd never seen before. Only then did Nero slow. He sucked in hard breaths, turning to look at me with a sheen of sweat on his brow. I inhaled hard, lifting my gaze to the towering buildings all around.

It was an alley, but like no alley I'd ever seen before. Bricked in verandas took up the top half of the buildings and every one of them looked into the courtyard.

"You live here?" I turned to him.

"I used to." He tugged my hand, taking me toward a set

of stairs hidden in the darkness. "Before my dad wanted me to learn the ways of the Pack."

We raced upwards, the cool wind reaching under my skirt as he laughed and then stilled at the top of the stairs. A woman stepped out of a brightly lit doorway, wiping her hands on a towel tucked into her waist. "I'd know that laughter anywhere. Come to me, *boy*."

Nero's hand slipped from mine as he strode toward her, and with each step he lowered his head and curled his shoulders. For a second I thought he was frightened of her; submissive.

And then as her arms went around him and pulled him tight against her I understood what it was...love. He loved her, and in her eyes he became someone else.

Not the blue-eyed cocky Wolf I knew.

But a *boy*.

A son...

This woman was his Mom.

"It's about time you came to see me." She ruffled his hair, checking the length of his curls and then flicked his ear.

"Oww! *What was that for?*" He reached up, and rubbed his ear.

"That's for not coming to see me sooner, and get a damn haircut, you're starting to look like your dad."

His grin was wolfish and consuming, bright sparks danced in his eyes. "That such a bad thing?"

"It is in my book," she warned, and then turned those careful eyes to me. "And who have you brought to my door, Nero?"

He jerked his gaze toward me. "Mom, this is Morwenna."

One brow rose on the woman's face. Silver hair sparkled

amongst midnight black as she strode toward me. "Morwenna have a last name or you want an old Witch like me to pull a card for that as well?"

I jerked my gaze toward Nero who flinched sheepishly.

"Livingstone, Ma'am," I volunteered and stepped forward, reaching out my hand.

She stopped two steps away, and caught her breath before she swallowed and glanced to my outstretched hand. "Well, that's one I never saw coming."

"We came for some information, Mom." Nero watched her. "Someone killed a Vampire in the tunnels and they want us the think it was a Witch."

She jerked her head toward him, and snarled. "Why?"

He just gave a shrug. "That's what we're here to find out."

She glanced at me once more and then snarled. "Better come in then. And wipe your damn feet!" She swatted the air near Nero's head as he passed.

He ducked, chuckled and then dragged his boot on the mat outside before stepping inside. I followed, making sure the bottom of my shoes were clean, before stepping into a brightly lit kitchen. Jars lined the counter, green and black colored glass sparkling under the overhead lights.

"Now, why in the blazes were the both of you in the sewers to start with?" She leaned over, grabbed a kettle and filled it from the tap in the sink.

Nero just glanced my way, leaving me to explain. I rolled my eyes, and mouthed, *thanks a lot.*

"I was looking for the Vampire," I murmured, looking around her kitchen. It was spotless and neat, except for the rows and rows of glass jars.

"Why is that?" She switched off the tap, and placed the

kettle on the stove before pressing the button, wait for the *poof* of the gas to ignite.

"He left something in my room, and I wanted to know why."

Nero's Mom turned and rested her hands on either side of her body as she stared at me. I could tell she didn't like me. I wasn't sure if it was because of my name or the fact that I was a Vampire. If I'd been anyone else, I would've been hurt. But I wasn't. I was a Livingstone, and we were used to being sneered at, scowled at...uninvited and unwanted, only until someone needed a service we could provide. Then we were their new best friend.

"And what would a sewer dwelling Vampire leave for a Livingstone?" She watched my every move.

I could lie...I could evade the truth. I could flat out tell her it was none of her business. I didn't owe her a damn thing. I glanced to Nero...

But I owed him.

Nero risked his life to get my ring back from the cat gang, and was awarded a kick in the balls for it. The least I could do was show his Mom a little respect, even if she was toeing the line of probing questions. I reached into the pocket of my jacket, grasped the soft felt bag and pulled it free. "He left this."

Her gaze narrowed on the bag. She said nothing before she pushed off the sink and crossed the kitchen. Her gaze roamed across the bag, but she made no move to touch it. "You said someone made the Vamp's death look like it was done by a Witch?"

"Yeah, but they fucked up. The corners weren't called, because they weren't connected. Whoever drew the pentacle didn't have a clue what they were doing."

"Amateurs," she snarled as the kettle on the stove started a soft whistle.

"But he was definitely dead, all shriveled and shit."

She tore her gaze from the felt bag in my hand and made for the sink once more. "All *shriveled and shit,* isn't an apt description, Nero. He might live in the sewers, but the creature deserved a little more than to die at the hands of a lying murderer. I don't know what your father's teaching you out there with the others, but it sure as Hell isn't reverence."

She pulled put out three tea cups from a cupboard and set them on the counter in front of her. Fingers danced across the metal lids of the glass jars before they stilled.

She unscrewed the caps, taking pieces of bark, and roots and other things I had no knowledge of before she dropped them one by one into the ceramic pot and filled it with steaming water.

Nero smiled. He seemed excited by the seeping brew.

"So, we have a Vampire, dead at the hands of a liar and a bag marked by Witches, filled with magic that shouldn't be in the hands of an inexperienced Vampire. No offence." She cut me a glare.

"None taken," I murmured.

But underneath I flinched from the sting. Part of me wanted to let her know how powerful this *inexperienced* Vampire was.

She grabbed the handle of the teapot, swirling it three times to the right and then three times to the left. "Is that magic, you casting a spell on me or something?"

Nero gave me a look that said *seriously?*

"No, I'm mixing the tea," his mother answered. "Something to relax you...you seem a little on edge, Vampire."

I gave Nero a look of my own...*your mother started it.*

He just shook his head, smothering a smile as his Mom turned and strode toward me with a cup half filled with dark green tea. "If I wanted to hex you, Morwenna, you'd be quaking like a damn duck and looking for somewhere to nest."

"Mom," Nero warned.

I still had the bag of diamonds in my hand, and the mere fact she never touched them made the jewels feel...*unworthy*. She gripped the cup and offered the handle. "Please." She motioned deeper into the room. "Take a seat."

Nero strode to the sink, grabbed the other two cups and followed as I walked into a small dining room. There was a round table there, four chairs tucked neatly underneath. Nero's Mom motioned to one as she pulled out a chair and sat.

I felt awkward around her...unsure of myself, and I was *never* unsure of myself. But Witches never mingled with Vampires, or Wolves for that matter.

Dad hated the Wolves, but he quietly feared the Witches.

"Drink your tea," she murmured.

I found myself lifting the rim of the cup to my lips and blowing on the steaming liquid before I took a sip.

Gross. Tasted like dirt.

Still I drank as Nero's Mom started talking. "I don't need to touch them to know what they are. They're magic, and not just run of the mill Witches magic either. They've been spelled, and the Witch that spelled whatever's in that bag is far more powerful than I am."

She reached out, curled her finger underneath the bottom of my cup and lifted, raising the rim to my lips once more. "Drink it all. Yeah, I know it tastes bad, but it'll protect you, as much as I can anyway."

I didn't know what she meant, still I swallowed as the hot liquid spilled into my mouth.

"Have you tried to get rid of them?" She leaned close and looked at the purple bag in my hand.

I just nodded. "They keep coming back. Dad says they've marked me."

She winced at the word. "Not necessarily marked, but drawn to you. Powerful magic surrounds them...but not necessarily you, and that worries me for a few reasons. There's a presence..." She held her hand over the bag. "It's dark and powerful...and very feminine. But it's hiding itself from me. But this...doesn't mean they have anything to do with the death of a Vampire, sewer dweller or not."

She stared into my eyes and under the sparkling overhead lights I caught the concern in her eyes. She never turned her head, but spoke to her son. "You need to be careful, close your own circle, you understand me?" She glanced at Nero. "Keep your friends close."

He just looked at me with a fierceness I'd never seen before and murmured. "I felt something the moment I saw the diamonds, and then again around the Vampire's body. Someone wants to start trouble with the races. Someone powerful."

His Mom turned back to me and with a cold, icy tone. "And it looks like they found the perfect target. You're powerful, Morwenna, and power can be a tricky thing, give too much to someone not yet ready to consume it, and it could destroy you. So, the focus for you must always be making sure you're strong enough to withstand it."

She rose from her seat with barely a sound. "My door is always open, if you have any questions, or you need a sanctuary. Us Witches who live here are no longer part of the

Blood Moon Coven, we prefer to think of ourselves as solitary sisters. But we'll protect you if you come to us."

I tucked the bag of diamonds into my pocket before she reached out, slipped a warm hand over mine. Maybe I had her all wrong, maybe underneath that bitter exterior there was someone who cared for me.

"And you." She whipped her gaze to Nero. "Tell that no good father of yours that my bathroom tap still needs fixing, and if he doesn't get his furry ass here in the next week, I'm going to find someone else to fix it for me."

Nero's cheeks burned bright red. He gave a nod and then rose to leave, before his Mom chuckled and reached out, ruffling his curls. I glanced around the small dining room that led into a lounge, and rose as well.

Black and white candles lined the mantelpiece above a well-used fireplace. There was a picture above it, dark, gloomy, blacks and blues, and a woman stood in the middle. Three actually, three versions of the same woman.

The clatter of a cup in the sink drew me back. I grabbed my own and strode into the kitchen as Nero's mom leaned in close and whispered something in his ear that only made him blush harder than before.

He cut me a glance and muttered something about. "Not the right time yet, Mom."

"When is there ever the right time?" she asked him.

He just shook his head and then glanced at me. "You ready?"

I wanted to say no, to enjoy the loving torture his mom was giving him just a little more, but I needed to get back and check on Ava. She was always a little seedy after eating a person, goodness knew how she felt after eating a Demon. "Yep."

He leaned close, gave his Mom a peck on the cheek before reaching for my hand once more.

"Don't forget about my bathroom tap," she called out as he towed me through the door and out onto the veranda.

"Got it the first time Mom!" he yelled.

The heavy sound of his boots rang out behind us. I glanced over my shoulder and raised my hand. "It's was nice to meet you, thank you for the tea!"

"Come to me if you need, Vampire," she called. "And be careful."

Her words resounded in my head as we ran down the stairs and then out into the courtyard. Her words stayed with me, like a weight around my shoulders.

I sucked in a breath as Nero slowed three blocks from his Mom's house. "You...you don't stay with your Mom when you're not at the Academy?"

He shook his head, his chest rising and falling with huge gulps of air. "Mom's a Witch and Dad's a Wolf. They tried to make it work, but it just ended with him baring his teeth at her, and her threatening to turn him into a rug for the fireplace."

"Seems like she still loves him."

"Oh yeah, they love each other, just can't stand to live together. Dad needs to run, and Mom...well...she needs solitude."

"And her bathroom taps fixed."

His cheeks went red again with the comment. I stopped walking and then turned with my hands on my hips. "Why do you turn beet red every time she mentions that."

"It's code," he mumbled.

"Code? Code for what?"

Nero shot me a glare. "What do you think?"

It took me a second, a whole second, before I felt the heat rush to my face. "Oh."

He chuckled even though he blushed. "Yeah, *oh*. Dad comes around when Mom calls, other than that they maintain separate lives. Witches and Wolves and all that."

One tug of my hand and we were walking again, hurrying along the city streets until we left the traffic behind. The familiar view of trees filled the horizon. Through the woods, lay Bestias Academy. It looked so strange from this view...so...*normal*.

We hurried, racing along the Academy road and then cut across the grassy area and slipped into the trees.

Branches snagged my jacket as we hurtled toward the grounds and then in an instant Nero slowed.

I inhaled hard, glanced around us. "What...what is it?"

He just leaned over, braced his hands on his knees for a moment before straightening. His blue eyes sparked with something akin to fear as he took the two gigantic strides and closed the distance between us.

He lifted his hand and cupped the side of my face, his voice husky with desire. "I've wanted to do this for so long."

And in a heartbeat he leaned close and kissed me.

I froze, unable to register anything but his hand on my cheek and lips against mine, moving deeper...hungrier. I found myself giving into him. Parting my lips for him as the kiss turned urgent. Nero moved closer. His chest pressed against mine, his hand fell to find the small of my back.

He held me against him...

I lost myself.

Until a twig *snapped*.

Nero flinched and pulled away.

I sucked in hard breaths as he searched the trees and then froze.

"Judas." That one word turned everything upside down.

My heart clenched tight, filling my chest with not a thud, but a flare of agony. I wrenched my gaze toward the movement finding Judas as he turned those pain-filled brown eyes from Nero to me.

CHAPTER ELEVEN

THE KISS THAT LED TO RUIN

"I expected her to betray me with the teacher, but not you," Judas snarled, the shadows darkening his sharp gaze, his attention locked on Nero and me.

Ice ripped through me as I stumbled from Nero's arms.

"Judas." I reached for him.

"Forget it." Judas stepped backwards, and that hurt more than any slap could. "Just forget it all."

He turned then, striding between the trees...taking a chunk of my heart with him. I glanced to Nero...who stared after the Alpha...lost.

"I don't understand," I murmured.

Deep down I knew I'd hurt him...*we both did.*

Nero shook his head, pain ravaging his blue eyes. "You did nothing wrong, Mor. This...this is all on me."

He took a step, leaving me standing there unable to process how I'd hurt him. "No." I strode forward, grabbing Nero's arm. "I don't understand what happened."

He lowered his head, shoulders curling in defeat. "Judas already told you. It's none or everyone with him. We never set the ground rules. I just figured that you and him would...oh Hell, I figured you'd go to him and then we'd be able to...but then today, I just...today with you and me, it just felt so real."

I swallowed hard, as the entire day raced through my mind. The water on my cheek, and the laughter ringing in my ears. "It was real. It was *all* real."

"And then I kissed you, and ruined it."

My mind was racing, trying to fit it all together. "So, he's upset that you kissed me before he did?"

Nero flinched. "No. *He's* hurt because we did this in private. I could kiss you all over and he wouldn't raise a brow, if anything he'd like it. But it was because we didn't do this with him and Bond, because this was *selfish*. And that's not the pack way."

Not the pack way, that was the second time I'd heard that.

My body was trembling as I lifted my gaze to the trees where Judas had disappeared. "I'll explain what happened. I'll tell him it was *my* fault."

Nero just shook his head and took a step away. "It wasn't...and it isn't. This is up to me to fix. Come on, I'll walk you home."

I opened my mouth to say something...*anything*.

I'd let the Wolves into my life. I didn't want to lose them.

Not now.

"Morwenna," Chuck growled, and I jerked my head up to find him marching toward me, furious and pumped up.

What now?

"Where have you been?" he barked, eyeing me head to toe, his gaze settling on my shoes smeared with mud, and then cut Nero a glare that could've frozen Hell itself.

"I think you should be good for the rest of the way now."

Nero muttered and glanced at Chuck before turning and leaving.

I didn't want to watch him leave...not when my heart was aching. Instead, I shrugged. "I'm just tired, Chuck."

I dragged my feet over the lawn to get rid of the mud.

"What happened?" He was at my side. "Someone hurt you?"

Hurt. Interesting word, no matter how honest this day started. I didn't mean for it to end like it did.

"Crazy day with the demon attack and all." I thought of Ava, realizing I hadn't spoken to her since she gobbled up one of the fiends to protect her love interest here. "You know Ava saved your ass back with the demons."

He cut me a hard stare and if I wasn't feeling so heart-broken, I might have laughed at him. "I could have taken them both on. But she's got incredible strength." And I studied the way the corners of his mouth twitched as he fought not to smile when he talked about Ava.

"If you shatter her heart, I'm gonna have to break your knees."

"She's too young for me," he muttered, but the icy tone didn't sound convincing.

"Yeah right." I marched ahead, neither of us saying a word at first.

Salome hurried past us, glaring my way, before she shoved through the dorm doors and disappeared inside.

"Come back with me," Chuck offered. "I've got tea."

"That's a first. A big bad Vamp who drinks tea. No thanks," I muttered stepping inside the dorm's front door. 'I'm all tea'ed out."

I shoved open the door to the dorm building and stepped inside, ready to shut it behind me, when Chuck's hulking form followed on my heels.

"You can't come in here."

One brow rose. "Wrong. I'm now permitted as long as I only enter your room or stand outside your door."

I sighed. Of course Dad would insist on stronger protection and Ms. Stone would cave to his demands.

"Fine." I had no energy for arguing.

I turned, pushed the door wide and made for the stairs. I shoved the key into my lock, and stumbled inside. Chuck never followed, instead he stood sentry outside my room. I collapsed onto my bed, feelings of loneliness and pain ravaged what little control I had. All I wanted to do was curl up on my bed and never leave my room again.

The Demons. Nero's first kiss.

Judas.

Why did everything have to always spin so out of control?

Strands of my hair tangled with the breeze and I turned my face towards the coolness. "Mmm, that feels nice." I opened my eyes.

Something sparkled through the curtains...I slid my feet from the bed. Diamond trees littered the campus grounds like elegant brooches. Just a dream, I tried to tell myself.

"It sure is," Mr. Leathers' sultry voice came from behind me.

I wanted to back away from the dream...wanted to rise to the surface of my consciousness.

"Not again," I warned. "I'm not here for you."

"Do you feel it?" he whispered moving closer. "It's so strong."

He chuckled softly behind me, enjoying himself. His hands fell to my waist, and I flinched at the unexpected touch. "*They took them you know? They took them but they didn't understand...they didn't understand the power that lay inside. But they will, won't they, Morwenna? We'll show them.*"

I didn't understand anything he said. "I don't think we should do this."

His arousal pressed against my ass, driving deeper as he rocked his hips forward. "*This is who you were meant to be.*"

The tips of his fingers skimmed my breasts. I squeezed my thighs together and shut my eyes. Blood thrummed through me with the heavy thud of my heart. I fell backward into his arms.

Needing him.

Desperate to have his hands all over me.

"*Embrace what you are,*" a female's voice insisted.

Startled, I snapped open my eyes and found myself wrapped in feminine arms.

I pushed against her limbs which were looped around my stomach. Where was Nefarious? "What are you doing?"

"*This is the only way,*" she insisted and lifted her hand, but this time instead of touching my body she gripped something in her fist. Light speared through the gaps of her fingers, and as she unfurled one finger at a time I saw it was the brightest diamond I'd ever seen.

"*They used it to summon me...but I was already here, already inside them. Until they took them...and gave them to you.*"

She shoved the stone against my chest. Electricity jolted through me, stronger than ever before.

I glanced down to a sparkle against my skin, and watched as it slipped inside.

"No, no, please no."

"It has to be," she murmured. *"God like...transcendence. Like, calls to like."*

I woke with a scream on my lips, my body vibrating until the quakes rattled the bed. I shoved the dream aside, and slapped my hand to my chest.

There was nothing, no mark...no goddamn diamond, no Nefarious and the strange woman.

I'm so sick of these damn dreams.

Outside, the morning sun was climbing over the horizon. "What the Hell?" Chuck must have left me after I dozed off. I'd never slept this long before either.

The dream felt so real, so damn terrifying. Nothing made sense. Not a single thing.

Shaking my head, I marched toward the bathroom when I toed something hard. I howled, the pain shuddering through me like broken glass.

"What the...!" I fell to my ass and held my throbbing toes, then spotted the purple near the bed.

The bag of fucking diamonds was back.

And I screamed with utter frustration, with fury because I *was* stuck in Groundhog's Day.

Before I could reach over to grab the culprit that might have crippled my toes, Ava tore into the room, her sleepy eyes wide, her blonde hair sticking in every direction, wearing her pajamas with tiny mermaids on them.

"You screamed?" She stared down at me, her fear morphing into sarcasm. "Did you just stub your toe?"

Then her gaze shifted to the bag and her mouth dropped open. "For the love of all things Poseidon. Fuck me!"

"We need to get rid of the diamonds. They're making me dream all kinds of shit." I hugged myself, trying to wipe the last one from my mind.

Ava marched over and snatched them off the ground, then stormed into the bathroom. "We should have done this the first morning you found them." The plonking of lots of stones hitting water sounded, then the toilet flushed.

Ava stood in the doorway holding an empty purple bag, smug, proud of herself. "These damn things have woken me way too early lately. Thank Hell they're now gone."

She flung the bag across the room, aiming for the trash can near my desk, but it missed completely and hit the desk with a heavy thud.

We both exchanged glances and rushed over. I snatched the bag with stones clinging inside.

"No way!"

"They're fucking cursed," she bellowed.

I fell onto the seat and poured the jewels onto the table, the diamonds rolling around, catching the sun. They had this gorgeous hypnotizing gleam to them, but they were so much more than pretty. "We should count them. Maybe there's some significance there. See if any have markings." I picked one up, rolling it between two fingers, studying how perfectly clear the stone was... not a blemish in sight.

Ava leaned over, poking the stones with a finger before picking one up, studying it. I started to count them. There was a total of thirteen stones, including the one Ava stuck between her teeth and bit down on, testing it for hell knows what.

A sudden knock at the door had us both flinching so abruptly, I broke out laughing, but Ava wasn't chuckling. She was cracking her chest, her mouth eyes bulging out.

"I swallowed it. I fucking swallowed a diamond." She was pacing in a tight circle, and I leaped to my feet and rushed to her side.

"Can you cough it up?"

She gawked at me. "It's in my stomach, not jammed in my throat."

The knock came at the door again. "Morwenna," Chuck called out.

Crap. "*Give me a sec, I'm naked.*"

"Is Ava naked too?" he asked.

"Eww."

Ava called out, "Wouldn't you like to know, big boy!"

I slapped her arm gently. "Not sure this is a flirting moment."

She rolled her eyes. "That's where you're so wrong."

"I can hear you," Chuck called from behind the door.

Ava moved closer and whispered, "Look, one stone's gone. It hasn't come back, so maybe this is a good thing."

Her belly rumbled loudly and we both glanced down at her stomach.

"That doesn't sound good."

But she didn't respond, and her face seemed to turn green. "Oh, shit!" She ran into the bathroom. "Stand the Hell back." The heaving sound of throwing up followed.

I cringed. "Are you okay?"

Chuck burst into the room, and I jumped. His gaze skimmed over me as if I didn't exist. "Where is she?"

I pointed to the bathroom, and went in there with him to find her gurgling water from the sink before spitting it out and wiping her mouth with my towel. Then she turned and opened her fist. In the middle sat a diamond. "This sucker isn't leaving your side."

"Eww, I'm not touching that." I stepped back as she glanced over at Chuck, both of them googly eyed, and I shook my head before retreating into the room.

"You okay?" He seemed genuinely concerned.

Hell, he was so smitten with her.

"Sorry, Mor." She slapped the stone onto my desk. "They're attached to you."

"I can take them to your father?" Chuck stared at the diamond.

"Won't do any good, they'll be back here in the morning." I pooled all the diamonds into the bag and left them there. Not as if they were going anywhere.

When no one responded and I suddenly felt like the third wheel in my own room, I waved at the duo. "Okay, out, if you're only going to gawk at each other. I'm getting changed and need... Hell, I don't know what I need. But it's not looking at you two."

Ava glanced at Chuck and then made for the door. "Meet you in fifteen." She darted from the room in her mermaid printed shorts and tank top pyjamas.

Chuck took a step toward the door and said, "I'll be waiting downstairs."

And then I was alone.

With the diamonds....

I reached up and rubbed my chest without thinking...and deep inside...under flesh and bone, something vibrated with energy.

Something pressing into the middle of my chest.

Something that made me feel alive.

CHAPTER TWELVE

YIELDING TO THE ALPHA

I COULD FEEL IT...THAT *TWINGE* INSIDE MY CHEST. I washed and scrubbed, lathered my hair and then rinsed, and every time I touched the middle of my chest I felt that buzz....

Something was in there...something that wasn't just a remnant of a dream. I dried, ran a comb through my hair and dressed. When I stepped out of my room I spotted Ava talking to Chuck, murmuring in a low voice, standing way too close.

"You ready." I glanced toward Nesrin's door out of habit.

"Good to go." Ava turned and then winced. She raised a hand and shoved a fist against her chest and let out the biggest belch I'd ever head. Chuck's eyes widened before his hand slipped into his coat pocket.

"Sorry," Ava muttered. "Demon." As though that one world explained everything.

"Here." Chuck peeled off two small white tablets from a roll. "These will settle your stomach."

Ava smiled and looked up at him like he'd just goddamn proposed.

I rolled my eyes and headed for the stairs, taking two at a time before I pushed through the dorm doors.

"Hey," Ava called, crunching on whatever Chuck had given her. "What's got you all riled up?"

I stopped dead in the middle of the pathway. Other students walked past, some turned and stared. I wanted to bare my fangs and hiss at them. I wanted to be the kind of primitive Vampire they expected with a name like Livingstone. But I did none of that. I sucked in a hard breath, feeling that burn inside my chest and tried to find the words. "I fucked up."

She picked at something her teeth and cocked her head. "What did you do?"

Tell her. The need raged inside me. I had to tell someone. I had to get this...*burden* out of my damn chest. "I kissed Nero."

"So?" She shook her head.

"No, you don't understand. I kissed Nero and Judas saw, and now he's upset 'cause I broke some stupid pack rule, and I feel like shit about it."

"Did you want to kiss him?" she asked.

I thought about it for a second, and I thought about *him*. I hadn't really given him much thought before, or Bond for that matter. It's just been *the Wolves*. The three of them went everywhere together. The three of them were always inside my head. But yesterday they weren't. Yesterday it was just Nero, and we'd laughed together, we'd been horrified together, we'd protected each other. Did I like him? "Yes, yes I did."

"Then I fail to see the problem here. If there's a pack

law that's been broken then that's not your concern. *You're not part of the pack.*"

But I want to be. The words raced through my head.

"Then if you want to be, make it work. Mend whatever hearts need mending, kiss whoever needs kissing and be done with it."

"Wait...you heard me say that? That I wanted to be?" I stared at her in disbelief.

"Ah, *yeah.*" She raised both brows. "You said it plain as day."

I'd thought it. But I hadn't said the words out loud.

"So, you going to sort it out, or are you going to stand there with your mouth open all damn day?"

My teeth gnashed as I slammed my mouth closed when out of the corner of my eye something scurried from the bushes and headed toward us. The demonic bunny was red-eyed and rabid, bounding across the grass until it lunged and with a hiss buried its tiny chomper-fangs into Ava's leg.

She squealed and kicked, dislodging the feral little beast mid-air. "I saved your ass!" she howled as the feral thing hit the ground in the distance and scurried away. "Ungrateful little gremlins!"

Chuck was there in an instant, hurtling his massive frame toward us like a locomotive to sweep Ava from her feet. But the beast had already scampered, tearing away from the sight.

I wish I was that rabbit.

Demon blood and all.

Ava giggled and swung her feet as he held her in his arms. I'd never seen Chuck look at anyone like that. His stony jaw bulged, dark, soulless eyes bore into hers. I could have a hundred damn henchmen racing for me in this moment, and he'd still be consumed by her.

"I think I just threw up in my mouth a little," I muttered as he lowered her feet to the ground.

There was a tiny scratch of blood on her leg. Still Chuck bent, swiped it with his finger and the stuck it in his mouth.

"She could be infected," I muttered.

"Very funny." Ava waved me away with her hand. "Off with you, *shoo!*"

I shook my head and smothered a smile. Even in the shittiest moods Ava knew how to make me laugh. I took her advice, lifted my head to the main building and made for the front door.

I'd make Judas listen while I apologized. Whatever it took, right? *Whatever it took.* I yanked open the front door and stepped around the other students milling in the middle of the corridor, catching sideways glances.

"What?" I confronted them. "What are you looking at?"

Still they never answered, only turned away. They hated me, *no*, they feared me, feared my dad, which felt the same to me. I reached for my pocket as a woman stepped out from the doorway of a classroom up ahead. She wore a black shroud, moving seamlessly like a ghost.

Like calls to like, Morwenna...this was...the only way.

I stopped dead. Letting some pimply Ghoul smack into the back of me. "Watch it," I snarled, unable to take my eyes from the classroom where the woman appeared. Goosebumps raced along my arms. I tried to move but my feet felt nailed to the floor.

"Mor?"

I flinched and wrenched my head toward Nero as he stepped around me. He glanced to the corridor and then to me once more. "You okay?"

I swallowed, and then nodded. "Yeah, sure."

But he wasn't, from the defeated look in his eyes to his slouched posture. He looked like he hadn't slept all night. I didn't know if that was better than the plague of dreams which haunted me.

"You okay?" I reached for him and caught the flinch before I dropped my hand.

"Yeah, yeah I'm good."

Lies. They slipped so easy from his lips. He wasn't, and he clearly wasn't in the mood to talk either. So, I didn't talk. Instead I reached for his hand and grasped his fingers with mine, before tugging him. My gaze went to the doorway, searching for the woman in the shroud as I strode along the hallway and passed, dragging Nero with me. But the woman never returned, even as I stepped around other students and passed the open door where the woman disappeared.

Ms. Lucas sat at the desk at the front of the classroom. She lifted her head, peering at me with beady demon eyes as I passed and towed Nero with me.

"Mor, where are we going?" he murmured.

"We're going to sort this out, once and for all."

I sucked in a hard breath and turned right. I knew exactly where to find Judas, we shared more than a friendship; we shared a darker need.

"I don't think..." Nero started.

"Then don't think," I said and headed for the classroom at the end of the hall. I inhaled hard, taking in the sweet, crisp scent of the moon. 13 Moons. The classroom was purpose built, silver walls, black furnishings. A hanging sphere in the middle of the room that held within it the power of the dark moon. It was a place of peace, a place where immortals like Judas could catch their breath.

There was no draining energy of the waning moon here.

No manic, consuming power of the full.

Only the peace and serenity of those three perfect days where everything floated to the bottom...and turned dark once more. Nero tugged his hand from mine as I slowed at the doorway. But I gripped him tight, dragging him into the room as the Alpha turned from the blacked out windows.

Judas' dark brown eyes met mine. But this time there was no spark of excitement, no curl of his lips. There was nothing but cold, stony pain.

"Judas..." I started.

The Alpha turned his back on us, cutting my words off.

The act hurt, more than I ever expected. I swallowed hard, trying to find my voice and glanced to Bond who lounged on a sofa in the corner. He watched me, and then glanced to Judas and back to me, like he was hopeful. We were all hopeful.

"It was my fault." I found the strength to take a step closer. "If you want someone to blame, then that's me. I could've said no. I could've pushed him away. But I didn't."

"No, you didn't. You did the one thing I said we were against. But this was not your doing, was it?"

Nero tugged his hand from mine, and this time I let him go. "No, it's mine."

"Pack rules," the Alpha sneered without turning his head.

I caught Nero's face turn ashen. "You want me out?"

I shook my head. No. This wasn't right. "No, *Hell no.* This is not happening. Not over...*over a goddamn kiss.*"

Judas just gave a shrug, and this time he turned to meet my gaze. "I told you this was how it's going to be...it's all of us, or none of us."

And he could just do that? Cast Nero out? God he was cold...cold and hard and *fuck me,* gorgeous. He never bowed, never yielded, did he? He just stood there looking relaxed and angry and pissed all in one. Messy curls pushed back from his face, letting me see every flare of dominance in his eyes. Letting me know just where I stood.

Heat flared, surging through my body, and unlike the dirty gross feeling from my dreams, this desire, I wanted. "You want me to choose right?"

There was a twitch at the corner of his eye.

"You want me to be all in or nothing. And then will you forgive Nero? Then can we move on, and get back to where we were."

He just shook his head. "We can *never* get back to where we were, Morwenna." He took a slow step closer, muscles ripping underneath his academy uniform. Brown eyes shone with a silver glare as he strode toward the moon in the center of the room. "I'm not interested in being played, nor is Bond. We *can* start from here, but I'm letting you understand, I want more."

I tried to breathe, tried to catch my thoughts. "More, more than what? More than being my friend?"

He just gave a shrug. "It's all or nothing, you choose."

"And how is that fair?" I cut Bond a glare. "And you want this as well?"

The Shifter just pushed from the sofa and strode toward Judas' side. "We've been telling you this all along. We like you, Mor. We like you *very* much, and yeah, Judas speaks for me."

He wants me to kiss them? All of them?

Voices crowded in from the hallway. Student. Teachers. All out there...they could walk in at any moment. Judas just crossed his arms...waiting. He was going to make me submit like one of his betas...heat flared through my cheeks at the thought. I couldn't catch my breath. Couldn't stop this quake carving through my body.

I swallowed hard, tried to find the steel in my spine and took a step closer. He tried so hard not to react. But I saw his eyes widen. I caught the rise in his chest. I listened to the thunder of his heart...racing.

He thought he was in control. He thought he was the *only* Alpha in the room.

He thought wrong.

He lowered his arms as I stepped close, the peaks of my breasts grazing his chest. "Is this what you want?" I reached up and speared my fingers through his hair.

His lips parted, sparks ignited in his eyes.

"Is this really what you want? You want me to beg?"

I clenched my hold tighter, yanking on his hair just hard enough to jerk his head.

"Yes," the husky word filled the space between us.

I rose onto my toes and brushed my lips across his. "Yes, *what?*"

His pulse spiked, body trembled against mine. "Please," he murmured.

A smile curled the corners of my mouth as I drove his mouth against mine, taking his breath...taking everything. Desire coursed through me, welling between my thighs. I kissed him until my lips burned, reaching out to pull him harder against me.

Hard muscles quivered and shook as he gripped my waist, driving his hips against mine.

And in a heartbeat I tore my lips from his, and then turned to Bond. "This what you want too?"

He just nodded, unable to speak a word. I reached out, grasped the front of his school shirt and dragged him closer. "What do you say?"

"P-please," he tripped over his words and stuttered. "K-kiss me."

"That's a good boy." I dragged him closer.

He was harder, hungrier, taking everything I had to give. Heavy hands slid around my waist and then slipped to the curve of my ass. Bond held me tight against him. Still I could feel the others in the room, and the pungent smell of a Wolf's desire followed.

I drew the scent in, until it flooded my lungs, and then I pulled away. Red lips, needy eyes. Bond leaned into me, his hand clenching around my ass as I let go of his shirt. Instead I gently pushed him away and turned to Judas. "We good now?"

The look of bewilderment in the Alpha...

I just smiled and caught Nero's smile. I gave him a wink. "So glad we got that figured out." Then I strode from the room.

"What the Hell was that?" I heard Bond murmur as I strode through the door.

"You sure showed her, Alpha," Nero chuckled. "You are definitely the Alpha where she's concerned...*not*."

"Boys," Judas gave a sigh. "I think I just got played."

CHAPTER THIRTEEN

FIGHT. FIGHT. FIGHT!

Holy shit! When had I turned into Ms. Dominatrix? I'd taken charge of three Wolves, one of them an Alpha, and now I burned up on the inside as the truth of what I'd done sliced through me. I'd trembled so hard when Nero first kissed me, and now... Look at me go. Ava would be proud.

With everything going on, I'd wanted stability... needed my Wolves by my side through whatever the hell was going on with me. So yeah, turned out I was a tiny bit dominating. Who would have thought? But it felt amazing.

Despite the confusion and seriousness of the diamonds, my dream, and even the dead Vamp in the tunnels, I smiled. Maybe something might go right for me.

I was fiddling with my shirt that had ridden up—naturally none of the Wolves had told me—when someone walked past me so close their shoulder knocked into mine.

I tottered backward, jerking my head up.

Nesrin sneered in my face before storming past. I should have said something back, showed her my strong side, but my words failed me when her two minions snarled, throwing me so much hatred someone might think I was a demon with horns. When in fact, they'd tried to kill me by stealing my ring. Who were the real monsters here?

I raked a hand through my hair, just in case I'd sprouted horns. Nope, just plain old me.

Shaking off the uncertainty, I pressed on down the hallway to my next class located in the gymnasium. *Etiquette.* I grimaced, picturing myself walking with a straight spine with books on my head. I wouldn't put anything past this school.

A short, sharp pain struck in the center of my chest and I rubbed it with a fist. What in the world had that dream been about? But I struggled to believe it was just that—a dream. They'd started with the diamonds, and it was funny coincidence that Mr. Leathers himself was new to the school too.

As I walked past his classroom, I stopped, picturing his intrusion, and fury bubbled in my chest like a cauldron. So, I backpedaled, then peered through the tiny window in the door. He was collecting a bundle of papers from his desk and neatly tucking them into a black satchel.

Before I could gather my thoughts, I thumped the door open with a palm and marched into the room, fire swallowing my insides.

Mr. Leathers looked up, surprise on his face quickly morphing into a smile.

"Hello."

"Stop coming into my dreams," I snapped.

Stiffening, his eyes widened incredulously. "Pardon me?"

I rolled my eyes. "Don't pretend you don't know. Just tell me why. What do you honestly hope to achieve?"

He flicked hair out of his eyes, shut his satchel in slow

motion, before rounding the table and sitting on the edge, his legs crossed at the ankles, arms folded over his chest. "Morwenna, I have no idea what you're talking about. But I think you'd better tell me what's going on."

Why was he acting so...so fucking nauseating? I was fuming, gritting my teeth. "You keep coming into my dreams."

His eye cocked as if he held back a laugh.

"I'm not fantasizing about you, okay. This is something else, something damn serious, and you keep appearing. T-touching me. Then last night you became a female and jammed something into my chest." Hell, when I said it out loud, it sounded like a damn fantasy.

I gripped my hips and waited for him to explain himself.

He ran a hand over his mouth. "Morwenna, I give you my word I've not bewitched you or your dreams. I'd never disrespect you in such a way, or your father."

And that right there was the reason I knew he spoke the truth. Daddy Dearest terrified most... in particular other Vamps. Plus, there was something sincere in Mr. Leathers' voice, his expression made me believe him. So, I wanted to believe him, told myself he was being honest.

So, if it wasn't him, why would someone impersonate him and want me to believe he was involved. Or was I just imagining the whole thing and having weird-ass dreams because the diamonds were affecting me? I'd been marked, Dad said.

Speaking of Dad. I thought by now I'd be raked over the coals, or grounded for the next five years at least after venturing into the tunnels. Maybe Chuck didn't tell him about the body?

I yanked my phone free from my pocket as an ache cut across my chest.

"You okay?" he asked.

I took a step backwards, rubbing the spot and winced. "Yeah, just..." I couldn't find the words and shook my head. "Got to go."

My message to Chuck hadn't sent. It still sat there with the red letters. *Failed to send. "Ugh! Can this shit get any more complicated?"*

But Mr. Leathers moved fast, the air shifted, blowing through my hair, and he now stood in front of the door, pulling it open for me.

"At our next session we'll talk about the power of dreams."

Yep, *I spoke too fucking soon.* Complicated was becoming my new best friend.

I nodded and shoved my phone into my pocket once more. I'd try to message Chuck again later. First I needed to get out of this embarrassing damn situation and stormed out into the hall and hurried toward the gymnasium.

Stupid. So stupid. Now he'd assume I had a crush on him.

With fast steps, I entered the gym where I found everyone standing in a double column, boys on one side and girls on the other, facing each other.

Ms. Whitecotton frowned in my direction. "Nice of you to finally join us. Hurry up and join your classmates."

If they were giving out year awards, Ms. Whitecotton would receive, Most Likely Teacher To Kill You With Her Stare!

"She's always late," Brylee snarled, standing halfway down the line.

I rushed forward and squeezed in next to Ava, who'd

waved me over. Bond stood across from us, winking, his blond hair shaggy around his strong face. I was totally smitten with all three of the guys, though there was no sign of Nero or Judas in class though.

A loud clap had me flinching and I turned to find Ms. Whitecotton at the end of the two lines, holding an armful of masks. She handed them out, starting with the guys. They put them on, and each resembled a wolf's face. Bond stared at me, his head lowering, his shoulders rising in a wolf attack posture, studying me like prey. Was that how he saw me? Was he thinking of our kiss back in the moon room because I sure was, my lips tingling at the memory, not to mention his hand on my ass. A zip of excitement raced down my spine, and all I could think about was being pressed up against him again.

Ms. Whitecotton cleared her throat and shoved a mask into my hands before moving on. Ava jabbed me in the ribs with her elbow.

"Stop drooling over him in public," she whispered.

I glanced around but only the cat gang stared at me with daggers in their eyes. What was their problem?

"Everyone put your masks on."

I stared down at mine. A deer. All the girls were innocent deer, while all the guys were predatory Wolves. Yeah, I could see where this was going.

"Most dances are steeped in tradition to appease the gods, whether it's a ritual to beg for rain for your crops, or to ensure a bountiful hunt, everything had a dance. As is customary at Bestias Academy, the Black and White Ball will include the Horn Dance."

Everyone broke into chatter and laughter; when the teacher blew a whistle, the sound deafening. I cringed and covered my ears.

"Silence," she bellowed. "The Horn Dance is about mimicking a hunt in the wild. Boys and girls will take five steps toward each other, then pass one another, shoulders brushing, then another five steps. Turn and repeat five times. Then the hunt begins and you will spread out in a circle, the Wolves chasing the deer round and round, and every third step must be a skip. Are you ready?"

Okay, didn't sound too hard.

"What are we doing first?" Ava nudged me as she was staring down at her phone, messaging someone while hiding behind me from the teacher. I tried to look at her screen and could have sworn I'd caught Chuck's name, but she shut it off and stuffed the phone into the back pocket of her school tailored pants.

Ms. Whitecotton blew her whistle again and I flinched. She hit a button on her phone and a folklore tune boomed from the speakers. Our line moved forward.

I fumbled with my mask and slipped it over my head, walking to catch up with everyone. Bond brushed past me, our shoulders grazing, his hand finding my ass. I gasped and coiled around to hear him laughing as he walked away. We spun and faced each other once again. We continued, back and forth, each time we passed, he pinched me, slapped me lightly, lifted his mask and blew me a kiss. I buzzed all over with excitement. A girl could so get used to this kind of dance. Ava was next to me making gagging sounds, but I bet she'd be all over Chuck if he was part of the dance.

Suddenly the music picked up in tempo, and the teacher blew her damn whistle. "In a circle, quickly. The wolves are hunting. Go!"

We all spread out into a wide circle, moving clockwise, and goddamn skipping. I was convinced if I were a deer running from a wolf, skipping wouldn't be involved.

Ava was ahead of me, giggling, enjoying herself. Across the circle was Bond, his eyes on me.

"Faster!" Ms. Whitecotton yelled and the tune sped up. She pumped up the volume.

Hell, was she insane? But everyone moved faster. One step. Two. Skip.

Quicker.

The music was like coffee injected right into my veins. I sweated, and yet we kept moving. I wasn't made for running from prey. Vamps were the hunters, Dad would say. Anger roared through me, or was it the desperate need to run, to escape danger right on my heels? Whatever it was, I was ready to go hunting.

"Faster!"

Fuck.

Someone kicked my feet out from under me and shoved a fist into my lower back.

I cried out, tripping over, and collected Ava with me on the way down. We both slapped the floorboards hard, gasping for air, sweating.

A loud cackle pierced the never ending drumbeat song. And I knew exactly who it belonged to.

My adrenaline was soaring, and I scrambled to my feet and swung around.

But I stopped, eyes widened. It wasn't who I expected.

No pause. Brylee lunged for me, a snarl curling in her throat. Pure fury flooded her eyes. So much hate when I'd never done anything to her. But I was sick of them pushing and pushing. It was time for me to push back.

I charged and met her aggression, both of us colliding and falling to the ground. Punches, kicks, claws raking down the side of my face.

An explosion of screams burst around us, coupled with the chant, "Fight, fight, fight."

A swift hit to my gut and the pain jolted through my body. Brylee pulled away.

I rushed off the ground and hopped onto her back, an arm looped around her throat.

She scratched at my arm, pulling my hair, struggling against me.

I bit back the pain of her nails in my skin.

The teacher was yelling, the music blaring, and Ava had jumped into the action, laying a loud slap across Brylee's cheek.

Everyone *ooed* and *ahhed* while Nesrin darted toward Ava, claws extended.

Except Ms. Whitecotton was there, blaring her fucking whistle in our faces, pulling on my arm and Nesrin's who had Ava in a headlock.

But I wasn't letting go of this bitch, I was tired of their attacks and insults.

Bond was at my back in seconds, his hands seizing my waist, prying me off Brylee. Trying to anyway, because I clung to her, my legs wrapped around her like an octopus.

"Enough!" the teacher yelled, then proceeded to call someone on her phone. But the masses were cheering, and we fought without power but with our hands and pure animalistic fury.

"Bitch!" Brylee hissed, her claws digging into my arms' flesh.

In a heartbeat, the light and music died, throwing us into a darkened gymnasium.

We all froze.

The walls groaned and trembled, the lights flicked on and off.

"Earthquake," someone yelled.

Bond ripped me off Brylee, who choked and gasped for air, glaring at me with the promise of retribution.

Bring it on.

She rubbed her face, a purple bruise the size of my fist already darkening around her eyes. And when she looked at me, it was different... there was something else beyond the hatred she held for me. Fear.

Ava shoved Nesrin aside before joining me. Us against them, encircled by students, while the room around us shook.

Only then did I notice Salome sat back and didn't join the combat arena. Since when did one of the cat gang have a conscience?

The door to the gym opened with a bang and Principal Stone marched inside, her boots thumping the wooden floor, her lips twisted into a grimace, her eyes darkened.

"Shit," Ava murmured.

"What the Hell now?"

CHAPTER FOURTEEN

IN THE DARKEST HOUR

THE WALLS STOPPED SHAKING....

The floor now solid under my feet.

But the claws marks on my cheek stung like a bitch. I lifted my hand, trembling fingers skimmed the pain coursing down my jaw and came away bloody. "You really are a bitch, aren't you?" I snarled at Brylee.

"I'm a fucking *cat!*" she howled at me. Curly blonde hair flying, green eyes wild. "And don't *you* forget it."

"That's enough!" Ms. Whitecotton snapped from across the room.

Bond stepped in between us, one hand splayed in the middle of my chest as Brylee snarled. She wasn't coming near me, not now...not ever. "You're losing your shit, shifter." I just shook my head.

Hate poured from those eyes, and I had no idea why. She took a step closer, meeting Bond's outstretched hand.

"Easy," Bond warned.

"You Vampires think you're so good, don't you?" Brylee snarled. "Let's see how long that lasts."

I looked to Nesrin, who seemed just as shocked as I was,

standing in the middle of the room. And I turned my head, watching Principal Stone marching closer. "Great…"

"Morwenna Livingstone," our Principal snapped. "My office…*immediately.*" I ground my jaw and glanced at Judas and then Ava.

"I'm coming too," she snarled.

"No, you aren't," Principal Stone snapped.

But my spunky best friend shoved her hand into her pocket and yanked out her cell phone. "I am…and I'm taping this, we're gonna plead the fifth and the fourth if we have to."

Principal Stone just looked at her. "You really are a little special, aren't you, child?"

Ava just flinched with the words. I could see they hurt, see the flare of pain before she swallowed hard and then straightened her spine. "Special enough to know what's right. Brylee started it, Mor was just defending herself."

"*I'll do the defending around here,*" Principal Stone roared. She took a step closer, and the moment she moved, pain flared through my side from the diamonds in my pocket.

"Oww," I muttered and dragged out the velvet bag from my pocket.

Principal Stone's eyes widened at the sight, darkness moved in, filling her brown eyes with Demon black. Her lip curled, white teeth shone under the overhead lights. "Give those to me." She took a step closer and snatched them from my grasp.

The diamonds brightened the purple bag, shimmering with a power of their own. Agony ripped through me as she gripped them in her hands. "Wait." I took a step closer. "I don't think you should—"

"*You* shouldn't think at all…" the Principal snarled.

She lifted her hand, and a dark demonic power coursed through the room, pinching along my flesh. Gasps and cries echoed all around me as the Principal hurled the bag of diamonds to the ground.

They hit the floor with a *thud*. The blow was a gunshot to my chest. I stumbled backwards and grasped my chest.

"Mor?" Ava's voice crowded in. "Mor, what's wrong?"

But I couldn't answer.

I couldn't do a thing other than slap my hand to my chest.

The diamonds sparkled in the bag as Principal Stone lifted her foot, the heel of her boot aimed at the center before she drove it down on the bag, smashing it right in the middle.

Crunch, the echo ripped through my head. My knees trembled, and then let go. I was falling before I knew, hitting the floor in a second. Hands gripped me, faces so close to mine.

Ava's...Bond....

Nesrin.

"Stop." The word was a croak as I shoved forward, reaching out to snatch the bag of diamonds from the ground. The Principal's foot lashed out, narrowly missing my hand as I dragged the diamonds toward me.

Energy coursed through me, shaking my bones, gnashing my teeth. My friends were there, grasping my arms, dragging me to my feet. But they shouldn't be here...they shouldn't be anywhere near...*me*.

The lights flickered as I slowly pushed from the ground.

"What the..." Ms. Whitecotton muttered.

Bulbs brightened overhead, burning white hot until they couldn't withstand the power, and in a heartbeat died...*thud...thud...thud....*

Ava lifted her gaze as darkness swallowed the corners of the room, and edged closer to us. "Ah, Principal Stone...I think you pissed something off."

The Principal just stood there and lifted her gaze to the light overhead as it quivered and flashed. But the diamonds were all I felt as inside the bag they slowly changed.

Gone were the shimmering stones, now there was...emptiness and darkness. My fingers trembled as I yanked the string binding the top and opened the bag. Power raced through my fingers as the faint shimmering glow inside the jewels petered out. There was a chip on one jewel, broken fragments clinked at the bottom, a remnant from the Principal's rage.

I lifted my gaze as rage tore through me. Darkness crowded in, but this time it wasn't from the lights overhead. It was *inside* me, right in the center of my chest. Right in the place where the Vampire power hummed...

A scream tore along the hallway. High-pitched and tortured, terrifying, and everyone inside the classroom turned their heads...*everyone but me.*

Power rippled through my body, shaking my hands. The diamonds weren't just diamonds anymore. They were funnels...pouring a foreign dark *hunger* into my body. I felt it spreading through me.

The scream from outside grew, male and female, shrill and snarling, and it echoed in the room.

"Brylee?" Nesrin called.

I turned my head as Brylee's knees buckled and she fell to the floor. She shuddered and shook. Fingers splayed against the hard floor. But her nails were changing, turning into wicked claws as fur raced along her arms. Her joints popped, bones snapped. She bowed her spine, muscles strained, tendons bulging from the sides of her neck as she screamed.

Then that scream turned into a snarl as she shifted in front of me.

Others cried out and hit the ground; Wolves snarled and gnashed their teeth, a Selkie slapped his fin against the floor...a Lion snarled and shook her mane. Nesrin tried to hold on, refusing to give into the power swirling in the room.

Bond fell, shaking and whimpering.

But it was me who Principal Stone stared at. It was me they all turned to, and the howling rage that filled my head. I could hear the thunder of hooves from somewhere outside the academy. Light flared from the diamonds in my hand and was swallowed by darkness as the diamonds turned ink black.

"What the Hell is going on?" Principal Stone snarled, but it wasn't Principal Stone anymore...it was a Demon. Black eyes like midnight stared at me from the creature.

"Mor," Ava whimpered. "Y-you c-can stop this n-now."

I shook my head and turned to find her convulsing as she changed. Bond was writhing on the ground in front of me, fighting the change. "I'm not doing this." I shook my head and glanced at the glinting midnight diamonds in my hand.

Lies, that word whispered across my head as the sounds of screams grew in crescendo.

"Stop it," Nesrin snarled, her voice deep, and guttural. "Stop this now."

A tentacle flew out from the corner of Ava's eye and slapped her across the face. "*You stop it,*" Ava growled as another arm flung out from under her skirt. She tried to grab them, tried to keep her modesty as another arm unfurled and hit the floor with a *slap.* "You did this...you and your fucking *friends.*"

And as the last bulb brightened overhead and gave a flicker Bond succumbed, falling to his knees as he tried to hold onto his mortal form. But he failed. Brown fur peppered with silver sprang out across his body as his nose turned into a snout.

Movement from the doors caught my attention and I turned to find Judas and Nero rushing in, their bodies shuddering, also affected. Their eyes were wild with fear, expressions full of questions.

Nesrin snarled and shook her long black hair as it shortened. "No... *Not like this.*" She wrenched her gaze to mine. Green eyes burned with fury. "I do *not* bow down to you."

But she did...*they all did.* Every one of them fell, all except for Ava who just stood there, balanced on thick arms. Blood red suckers pressed against the floor. The markings raced along the side of her shimmering, pale face. Blue eyes turned black as she grew in size, pushing upwards and outwards, until she commanded the room.

And still this dark power swelled inside me.

Like it was limitless.

"Mor,' Judas snarled. He was on his knees, staring in horror as Nero shifted beside him. Black fur swallowed his beta, white fangs showing as he snarled.

Agony filled me as the sight of the Alpha fighting the change as Judas lifted those silver eyes to mine. Everyone else in the school had shifted, turned. I knew it without question, just as I knew the diamonds were not just a power...but a *conduit* for power.

And it was this power that filled me...*consumed me.* It was this power I felt in the height of the dream, when the woman pressed the diamond into my chest. I lowered my gaze, finding the flicker of *something* against my heart. Power burned. Power trembled. Power *rippled*.

"Mor," Judas snarled and gnashed his teeth. He was changing, pale pink skin darkening with fur.

I didn't know how to stop it, how to do anything but swallow, and swallow this energy. *No,* I roared inside my head and the sunlight of my Vampire powers pierced the darkness. *No more!*

And at the height of the tsunami of terror...the wave crashed.

Screams stilled.

Snarls turned into whimpers and fell silent.

The entire room seemed to collapse, even the Demon that was Principal Stone wobbled on her feet, before she crumpled, hitting the ground with a *thud.*

Even Ava. I glanced to her as she shoved out a hand and sank to the ground.

I stared at Judas who held onto his mortal form. He'd already started to shift...already had that glazed feral look of *hunger* in his eyes.

"I'm sorry." I dropped to my knees as the diamonds turned from black to sparkling clear once more. I shoved them back into the pouch then into my pocket. "I didn't mean..."

"*You...*" Principal Stone gasped and lifted accusing eyes to mine.

The rest of the classroom turned to stare at me...even Ava. A look of sadness and pain tore across my best friend's gaze before love pushed in. She shoved her foot against the floor and scooted toward me.

"Are you okay?" Judas croaked and lifted his head.

There was still a shine of silver in his eyes, still his *Wolf* waiting just under the surface. Nero shoved against the floor and pushed to hands and knees as he made his way closer. Bond did the same. All three of the Wolves and my best friend reached for me.

Warmth skimmed across me as they gripped my arms, my legs. Judas dragged me closer, pulling me into his lap as tears blurred my vision.

"I don't know what happened." I gripped his shirt, holding on as tears slipped down my cheeks. "I couldn't stop it. I couldn't..."

"Shhh," he whispered, his voice husky and raw. "It's okay now, you're okay, we're okay..."

Sounds echoed from the hallways. Husky, terrified murmurs. Slow, stumbling steps. Movement came from the doorway as Nefarious Leathers stumbled in, looking disheveled, startled. He glanced around the room and then settled on me. "Morwenna." His frantic gaze searched my hands, and then settled on my jacket pocket. "The Ancient," he stuttered. "The Ancient is coming."

I swallowed hard and then pulled away.

The Ancient was coming.

To see me.

Because of what I just did.

I looked to Judas, trying to find the truth in his eyes.

I didn't think it was okay. Not anymore.

CHAPTER FIFTEEN

ANCIENT MIDNIGHT

"I won't call your father on this incident," Principal Stone snapped, stiff as a board behind her desk, her cheeks red, her normally perfect hair ruffled around her face.

Everything about her was ruffled.

She glared my way.

Incident? Yeah right. More like she didn't want another *incident* of my Dad.

"This is your last warning," she started. "I won't allow my students to break rules and put others in danger."

"Rules?"

"Silence," she barked. "Being the daughter of the Master Vampire does not give you a free ride here. One more incident and you're out of the Academy." She almost snarled when she said the word *Vampire*. Wasn't she supposed to be impartial to all races as the Principal? Yet she stared at me with so much hatred. It wasn't as if I could control what happened in the gymnasium. It shocked me as much as everyone else.

Ms. Stone patted down her hair and dug for something inside the top drawer of her desk. She popped open a small bottle with shaky hands and tapped out two aspirins. Without a word, she threw them into her mouth and chased them down with several gulps of water from her glass. Demons felt pain, huh? That was a new one for the books.

"For now, it's best you keep the diamonds with you," she hissed.

I shifted in my seat, the bag of diamonds bulging from my skirt's pocket. Power buzzed and hummed through my veins.

I could still see the silver shine in Judas's eyes. Still see the fur swallowed by Nero's body.

Still see Ava slap the shit out of Nesrin with the tip of her tentacle.

All because of the diamonds.

All because of me.

How *did I do* that? How in the world had the diamonds affected me or forced everyone else to shift into their supernatural forms?

I do not bow down to you! Nesrin's snarl filled me.

I sat there, waiting for the punishment for what I'd done. I didn't want anyone to bow to me. I didn't want this at all. But it seemed someone did. Someone far more powerful than I was. My hand slipped to the bag of diamonds.

I just didn't want any part of it.

"Why are you still here? Off you go," Principal Stone snapped without meeting my gaze.

I pushed the chair back and rose.

"Stay in your room for the remainder of the day. Think about what you did." Her fingers fluttered at the side of her temple.

"Fine," I muttered. I'd think all right about how unfair she was being.

The bright sun beat down on me as I strode from the building and headed to my dorm.

I kept my gaze to the ground, not making eye contact with anyone I passed, and shoved through the door to my dorm.

I swiped my card at the vending machine and grabbed two vials of blood. I still didn't fully trust the stuff, taking a taste before I drank anything, every single time. Seems like trust was becoming the theme of my damn days.

I trudged upstairs and slipped into my room, dumping the blood and the diamonds on my desk and stared at the purple bag. "Why the hell are you in my life?"

Nothing made sense. The only thing that came out of any of this was more damn haters.

I snatched the first vial of blood, tasted it on the tip of my tongue and guzzled the rest before reaching for the other. Then I flopped onto the bed not wanting to leave my room ever again.

I kept myself busy and tried not to look at the bag of diamonds for the rest of the day. Instead, I sat outside on the balcony with textbooks piled on my lap. Still, I couldn't stop the thoughts sprouting like damn weeds inside my head. Finally, I shoved the Demonology manual aside and sighed.

I wondered what the Ancient would say? And why the Hell was he coming here? It couldn't be from what happened today, I mean, how could he know? Surely word didn't travel that fast.

My phone chimed with a message, and I headed back inside to find it buried under my papers on my desk

Ava: *Stone said I can't visit you today. Want me to climb onto your brûlée?*

What the fuck! I reread her message and shook my head, convinced she was the one losing her mind not me.

Another text.

Shit! Stupid autocorrect

Brûlée

Brûlée

Ahhhh I'm going to throw this piece of shit

I burst out laughing, still having no idea what she was going on about, but I loved that she still managed to make me laugh. And I typed my response.

If you come over, bring me a blood brûlée LOL.

Seconds later she responded.

Balcony. Fucking stupid balcony. I'm gonna climb your brûlée! Gah, I give up!

I exploded with laughter, holding my stomach as it hurt so much in the best possible way.

Next thing, my door opened and Ava slipped inside and shut it as if she'd been chased. She turned and eyed me with a smirk. "I can hear you howling with laughter from downstairs."

"Did you bring my *brûlée?*"

She chuckled and stuffed her cell phone into her pocket of her white school shirt. She rushed over to me, and without a word, collected me into her arms.

"How are you?"

I melted against her, loving how much she cared, and despite me being some kind of monster, she wasn't afraid nor did she pull away from me. "Considering I just forced everyone to shift against their will, and now I'm hated more than I was before, pretty damn good." I pulled back and she sat on my table, her legs swinging.

"I don't hate you," she muttered. "I've been looking for a reason to shift and slap some sense into Nesrin."

I chuckled, and shook my head. "This is supposed to be serious. I'm having a goddamn crisis here...what's everyone saying?"

She just shrugged. "Who cares about them. You're powerful, girl, and the rest can quake in their boots."

My stomach churned. "The gossip is that bad?"

She looked away, and shrugged. "It's subjective."

I didn't need the words. I heard them in the way her shoulders tensed and she swallowed hard. "I'll be okay." I reached across and grasped her hand.

A quick knock came at the door and we both jumped. Ava hopped down and darted into the bathroom.

"Who is it?" I hurried across the room.

"Just us," Judas called through the door.

I hit the lock and opened the door. Desire flared in my chest as Judas stepped inside, took a look around and settled those dark brown eyes on me. "We were worried," he whispered and reached up to tuck a strand of hair behind my ear.

I shivered at his touch as Nero and Bond pushed past and strode into my room.

"Heard you're under room arrest." Nero stilled and then turned.

My heart gave a shiver as he slid his hands around my waist and pulled me against his body.

For a second I froze. *Touch. Contact. Power. Diamonds.*

Didn't they know I was dangerous?

"We wanted to see you," Bond murmured as Nero lowered his head to nuzzle my neck.

"Is this okay?" Nero whispered.

I tried to swallow, tried to think. Tried to do anything but panic. I reached up, sliding hands around his neck as he pressed me harder against him. Nero radiated heat...they all did...pressing in from the other sides.

"You were seriously kickass." Bond slid his hands lower, against my hips.

"Hey, no smoochies while I'm here," Ava snapped, with a raised brow.

She came out of the bathroom and the boys pulled away. Shivers raced through me without them.

"I'm sorry." The words fell from my lips. "I don't know what happened."

Judas was shaking his head, confusion filling his gaze. "Don't apologize."

"It's those...those *things*." Ava pointed to the purple bag of diamonds on my desk. "They are *not* diamonds. That's all I know."

She was spot on. Ever since they arrived in my life, everything went to shit.

"The Ancient's bound to tell you what's going on." Bond's fingers were on my arm, stroking me, calming the worry knotting in my chest.

"That's not what I'm worried about," I admitted. "It's that he'll say the diamonds' mark can't be fixed. What if I'm attached to them for life?"

"Then you'll have to turn them into a massive diamond ring," Nero joked, chuckling at the notion of such a massive jewel.

"Holy shit, Nero, are you talking about an engagement ring? You only just met Mor!" Ava gripped her hips, glaring at the Wolf, whose eyes doubled in size as he turned to glare at her.

"What are you talking about?" he blurted.

"Diamonds. Ring. *Hello?*"

Judas and Bond broke out laughing, while Nero's gaze flicked from me to Ava, finally settling on me. "If it's what you want."

I raised my hand. "Stop. I'm honored, but she's joking."

Judas slapped Nero's shoulders playfully, then took him into a man hug, and they broke into roughhousing.

"Think we need snacks," Ava determined, and Bond nodded, then headed out the door.

"Shit," Ava neared me, whispering. "He was gonna—"

"No, he wasn't. You freaked him out. Don't say shit like that."

She smirked and wiggled her eyebrows with every intention to never stop saying crap like that. Before long, Bond returned with an armful of snacks including several bottles of blood. Damn, he was a keeper. We all rushed over to him, taking food before settling down, me with Judas and Bond on the bed, while Nero sat on my chair and Ava sat back on the table.

Yep, something about being surrounded by friends eased the agony tearing through me as I worried about why the Ancient wanted to talk to me. But that was later tonight. For now, I'd enjoy myself and pretend I was anything but the freak in the room.

"You sure this is where the Ancient wants to meet?" I faced Nefarious.

The wind blew his hair over his face, and he kept pushing it out of his eyes. His long black coat billowed behind him, mimicking a cape.

"Yes."

I glanced down from the flat roof of the cafeteria, two stories high where the wind whipped around my arms. The Academy grounds below were swallowed by night, trees rustling all around. I stifled another yawn and hugged myself.

"Would have made more sense to meet him in an office. He seemed fond of sitting by the fire back in his mansion, swirling a fine glass of wine. That seems more his style than standing on a roof in the middle of the night."

"Vlad Vasile does have a liking for bloodwine, especially the virgin variation." Nefarious' eyes bored into mine. My breath caught, remembering how I'd marched into his class and accused him of invading my dreams.

An inferno climbed up and over my cheeks, thank goodness it was night. But I believed him when he said he had nothing to do with them.

Someone cleared their throat behind us, and we both snapped around to find a tall, dark figure across the roof from us. His long cloak and dark hair weren't discernible in the darkness surrounding us.

"Lord Vasile, welcome." Mr. Leathers bent at the waist, his head low.

I stood there, unsure if I had to bow as I'd never seen Dad do it, but I followed my teacher's guide and gave a quick tilt of my head.

Vlad slid forward as if he were made of shadows. There was a reason he was in charge. As an Ancient, he was one of the few who retained the strong abilities, like shifting, morphing into mist. Dracula movies made it seem like all Vamps carried those traits, except only the oldest and most powerful Vampires had them.

"Child, did you bring them?" His voice was so rough and deep, it lifted the hairs on my arms. He resembled nothing of the laid back, talkative Ancient I'd spent time with at my first Understudy meeting.

All I could do was stare at how his eyes seemed to glow yellow beneath the moon's silvery hue, how red his lips were, the fullness of his cheeks. He'd recently fed on fresh blood.

"The diamonds," Nefarious spoke impatiently, staring down at me.

I fumbled, pulled out the velvet bag and handed them to the Ancient.

I didn't move, I couldn't. While I waited for his prognosis, I could only assume he'd heard about everything from Nefarious.

"Your power is incredible." The Ancient just stared at me. His tongue slipped out and slid over his lower lip before vanishing into his mouth. "I tasted it when you used it."

A shiver crawled down my spine, and I lowered my arm, still holding the bag. "Pretty sure it used me."

"But you're too inexperienced, too rash, too... What's the word?" He clicked his fingers.

"Naive?" Nefarious said after a moment of silence, and I cut him a hard stare.

"Leave us," Vlad's voice boomed like thunder in the air. With a wave of his hand he dismissed my teacher.

"Credulous," Vlad hissed between clenched teeth. "You believe too easily. Everyone is the enemy, Morwenna." He clucked his tongue at me. "Letting a sewer dweller into your room. What if he wanted to really cause you pain?"

"He needed help, and—"

"Don't you know anything? *Never* invite a Vampire into your home. Your father should've taught you the basics."

I winced at the words remembering how dad said the

exact same thing. My mouth opened with a response, but Vlad placed an icy, cold finger to my lips.

I tried not to gag. Instead I tried to remember who I was dealing with.

"There's a great power inside you. Something I hadn't felt before, and it needs taming. But first we must deal with this mess."

He made a light groaning sound, and shifted the bag to his other hand. "What is this?" He whispered and plunged his fingers inside. But in an instant, he hissed, and yanked his hand out, removing his ring and tucked it into his pocket.

"Is everything okay?" I asked.

He didn't respond, just poured the diamonds onto his palm. They glittered beneath the moonlight, but before our eyes, they lost their sparkle and dulled, darkened to a red.

Vlad grumbled deep in his chest, shifting on his feet.

His hand trembled as we both watched the stones now morph into pure black. He stumbled, his fist closing around them, his eyes shut.

As the diamonds touched his hand something savage and consuming tore through me. My heart gave a *thud*, and squeezed every drop of black blood into my veins. "My Lord..." I started and lifted my head. "I don't think you should."

He turned those ancient eyes on me. "You don't think at all, Morwenna. Not until I tell you to."

He touched the gems, moving them around in the middle of his palm. The more he touched them the more the unease inside me grew.

"I can't quite touch the energy inside them." He murmured, digging a hand into his pocket and retrieving the ring before slipping it over his index finger.

"What am I supposed to do?" I pleaded, suddenly feeling like the darkness was a noose around my neck.

"Keep the diamonds close. I've never felt such a power before."

"I'll instruct Nefarious Leathers to refocus your teachings on controlling power until I uncover what you're dealing with."

"But—"

He spun and glided away, vanishing into the dark.

"Hello? Are you still there?" What the hell?

"You done?" Mr. Leathers asked, his voice so soft, I jumped and whipped my gaze around.

"Shit, you scared me. Did you hear what he said?"

"Enough. Come, let's get you back to your room, and we'll start tomorrow on a new approach."

I followed him across the roof and toward the door, dread coiling around my chest like a straitjacket. How could no one know what was going on with me or what the diamonds meant? There were clues here and there, like the dead sewer dweller, demon blood near his body, my dreams and power, but I still couldn't piece it all together, couldn't figure out who was responsible and why. Exhaustion washed through me, and every inch of me suddenly ached.

What I needed was a long sleep, then maybe I could figure this all out. The only thing I knew for sure, was the power of the stones was growing.

Where it ended, I didn't know.

I slipped inside my room and didn't even both to change before I collapsed into bed.

WEEKS PASSED since my meeting with Vlad on the roof in the middle of the night.

He hadn't come back with a solution yet. Dad found nothing but insisted he was working on it. Classes went on as normal. I slept every moment I had a chance, constantly exhausted. I put it down to the growing pile of homework.

But all around me Vampires were getting sicker.

"You think he's left?" Ava murmured.

I lifted my gaze to the door of Chuck's little cottage, and bashed my knuckles on the wood once more. "Chuck, it's Mor. Are you in there?"

I leaned closer, catching a faint moan and dropped my hand to the doorhandle. "He's in there."

One hard twist, the lock gave, leaving the door to swing inwards.

"*Yoohoo!*" Ava called out and butted into my back.

"Ava," I warned stepping into the small living room and glanced at the neat little place.

"Oh man, what is that stench?" Ava gagged and then pinched her nose. "Smells rotten."

The foulness hit me. It did smell rotten...specifically rotten blood.

A moan came from somewhere along the hallway.

I glanced at Ava. "You might want to stay out here for this."

She just shook her head while pinching her nose. "It's okay, I'm all good."

I sucked in a breath and held it as I made my way to the bedroom at the end of the hall, and found Chuck crouched in the corner of the room.

Sunlight cornered him in the room. The pale light spilled across the top of one foot and the hiss of burning flesh filled the room. "Jesus," I muttered and then wrenched my gaze to the open blinds.

"Stuck," he muttered. "Too weak to fix."

I lunged for the blinds while Ava scurried toward him. His ring wasn't working. I stared at his hand, and then glanced to the tin on mine. His ring wasn't protecting him at all.

There were spent packets of blood everywhere, littered across the floor and over the unmade bed.

But the blood had found its way back in the bucket at Chuck's side. I yanked the blinds, tearing the heat from his foot and ending the hiss of burning flesh.

"Oh, Chucky," Ava cooed.

She didn't hold her nose anymore. Instead she glanced into the bucket and turned green. "Oh, okay, that's rank."

She grabbed the bucket and held it out as far as she could and raced for the bathroom.

I closed all the blinds and then hurried to his side. "How long have you been like this?"

"A week, I think," he winced and dragged his foot out from underneath his body.

The toilet flushed, and the sound of retching followed.

Rotting blood was bad anyway you saw it, especially one that had been regurgitated.

"Okay," Ava gasped and braced herself on the doorway. "Nope, I'm not."

She disappeared once more, and more gruesome sounds followed.

"Come on," I grabbed his arm and lifted. He was slick with sweat, trembling and weak.

"Don't...don't want you to see me like this."

I shook my head. "Nonsense. Being sick doesn't make

you any less the Vampire you were last semester when you carried me all the way home."

He stumbled to the bed and flopped down. Springs howled, sodden sheets wet from sweat stuck to his legs as he dragged them higher.

I tried to make him as comfortable as I could, but the truth was I couldn't.

Not until I found the cause for all this.

And stopped it.

CHAPTER SIXTEEN

WITCHING HOUR

I TRIED TO GET THROUGH THE DAYS AT SCHOOL, ignoring the sideways glances from the students and teachers. I trudged through classes, one after another. I barely ate, barely slept. My eyes were grainy, senses on fire. I flinched at every slap of a book and cried out at every chime of the class bell.

"You look like that," Ava murmured and jerked her gaze toward the image of the seven levels of Hell the whiteboard.

"Thanks," I murmured and licked arid lips.

I did feel like Hell. Worse than Hell actually. I blinked and tried to focus on our Hallowed Grounds teacher, Mr. Peace. But his voice droned.

I shook my head, trying to find a fragment of concentration and felt the notebook underneath my hand slide along the table.

"Easy," Judas lashed out, catching my notebook as it fell.

He cast a concerned look at Ava and then watched me.

"Eyes up front please, Mr. Blackthorne."

Judas straightened, curling his lips as he glared at the teacher. I swallowed hard and placed my hand on the book, making sure it went nowhere. But inside I was sweating. Inside I was terrified. I was losing my power, losing what made me a Livingstone.

My gums ached, I pressed the tip of my tongue to the swollen flesh and the pain tore through my skull. Something was happening to me, something in the weeks since I forced everyone in the school to turn into their beasts.

But this...sickness wasn't just mine. I turned my head and fought the wave of nausea at the movement. Other Vampires looked ill too, paler than usual. The undead hunters of the night were all growing weak, and none of us knew why.

I tried to listen to Mr. Peace, tried to capture his words, but in my head all I saw was the sewer creature, hidden in darkness, alone.

My door is always open, if you have any questions, or you need a sanctuary. Nero's Mom's voice filled my head. I sucked in a breath as my mind wavered. Still I clung to the thought, stopping it from slipping away.

The Witches...the Witches could help us. There was a curse on us, it had to be... what else could affect all the Vampires at this school?

Inch by inch I turned my head, but it wasn't Ava or Judas I searched for...it was perfect blue eyes...*Nero.* He cast a careful glance my way, his brow narrowing, attention consumed by me.

You okay? He mouthed the words.

I tried to nod, tried to move my head but I couldn't. I was consumed by thoughts and pain.

The shrill sound of the bell cleaved through my head, making me whimper. Judas pushed from his chair. "That's it, I'm taking you back to your room."

His gaze darkened to steel, hard, unbending. "Nero," I murmured. "Maybe Nero can."

There was a flinch from the Alpha, and in this moment, we teetered on the pain from weeks ago when he found Nero kissing me in the dark. But then Judas just nodded. "Okay, you take care of her, Nero. Whatever she needs."

I licked my lips and reached for Judas' hand. "Thank you."

Fear filled his eyes. He was worried...they were all worried.

Footsteps consumed my head as the students fled to their last class of the day. Bond moved, and Judas stole a breath and stepped closer. His lips burned against my cheek; breath just as hot. I swallowed the flinch as he pulled away, and then turned and strode from the room.

Ava was last, forcing a smile that was sad and pathetic.

"I'll be okay," I muttered. "Just need to rest."

She left then, giving Nero a glare and followed the others.

"Right, to bed with you," Nero murmured.

But I just turned my head slowly, forcing the pain underneath the desperation. "No, that's not why I need you."

One brow rose. He glanced to the others leaving and then turned to me. "What are you up to?"

"Your mom." My words were hoarse and raw. "I need you to take me to see your mom."

Sparks danced in his eyes. "You want to see a Witch?"

I nodded. The more I thought about it, the surer I was. She told me I needed to be strong, and if this was being strong...then I was failing miserably. She had answers. I knew she did.

"Meet me out front." He touched the back of my hand, drawing my attention. "Can you do that?"

I nodded and gripped the table as he left. I grabbed my notebook and snagged the strap from my backpack off the chair. The room spun as I slowly made for the door. I still held on with everything I had and slowly followed.

Sunlight pierced through the clouds and stung my eyes. I winced and yanked my hand upwards. But the sun tingled over my skin.

The car was a dark blur at the edge of my vision. The engine roared, and then slowly died as Nero pulled to a stop in front of me. He shoved the driver's door open and raced toward me with a heavy leather jacket in one hand and a pair of sunglasses in the other.

I stared at the sleek sports cars and then lifted my gaze to him. "This your car?"

He threw the jacket around my shoulders and slid the sunglasses gently onto my face. Darkness consumed me, and I lifted a shaking hand to his. "Thank you."

The jacket smelled of Judas; deep and powerful, and every bit of an Alpha.

"No, this is Judas', but today it's ours. Come on quickly before Ms. Stone comes out," he murmured.

I followed, climbing into the passenger's seat as he raced around to the driver's side and slid inside. With a slam of the door, we were off, pulling away from the front doors of the academy, and heading toward the main gates.

"Last time we did this we were looking for clues," Nero murmured and cast a careful glance toward me. "What are you looking for now?"

I swallowed hard. "The truth," I answered as he turned the car left at the gates, heading toward the city. This was more than a surge of power, more than the poisoning of blood.

Someone was out to hurt Vampires.

And I needed to understand who.

The diamonds clinked and rattled in my pocket. I couldn't bear to look at them now and didn't want to touch them. But if I was away from them for any length of time the pain only grew worse. So, I resigned myself to shoving them back into my pocket.

I settled into the seat and gave myself over to Nero. He'd take care of me...all my Wolves would take care of me, and Ava. I reached out, placing my hand on his thigh. "Thank you."

He cast me a panicked glance and pressed the accelerator harder. This...connection we shared was evolving, moving deeper the more time we shared. Judas and Bond were protective, sometimes battling each other for who guarded, and who protected. But with Nero it was different, he was careful, quiet, and controlled. He saw things the others missed...

He lowered his hand to mine on his thigh. "We'll work this out."

"It's because of the diamonds, Nero." I felt sick with the words. "It's all because of the diamonds."

He turned the car again, and then punched the accelerator, pushing me back into the seat as we sped toward the towering skyscrapers of the nearby city. But we weren't going to the glitz and glamor of high-end boutique stores like I was used to, and the more I thought about it the more I realized that was the old me.

I wasn't that person anymore. It didn't matter how many carats you wore, or which designer was creating your outfit. Hell, I was friends with Ava who called Chanel,

"Channel." I winced with the thought and smiled. She always made me laugh, even when we were miles apart.

We drove for a while and already, the afternoon sky dimmed.

"Almost there." Nero turned the car, heading to the darker, quieter suburbs.

Familiar sights of seedy buildings and darkened alleys filled my view. Nero hit the turn signal and pulled the car hard up against the curb. I lifted my gaze to the familiar brick building and the entrance to the courtyard.

Nero was out of the car in a second and rounded the front to open my door. I clenched my jaw and blinked behind the sunglasses as I climbed onto the pavement. "I hope she's home."

"There's only one way to find out." He shoved the car door closed behind me.

Every step was agony, but the shadows of the entrance soothed the sting of the sun. I glanced up to the balcony as we entered. But I couldn't quite see her door.

"Let me run up." Nero lunged and raced for the stairs, and I lost sight of him around the corner.

"She's not home." An old woman's voice murmured behind me. I turned to see a silver-haired woman step out of the shadows. Dark eyes gripped mine as she moved forward. "Take off your glasses," she commanded.

I reached up, slipping the shades from my eyes.

She was slow and hunched. Gnarled fingers reached upwards, sliding the sides of her fingers down my face. "You're sick, power sick," she murmured. "What's your name?"

"Morwenna," I murmured.

"Your last name, child," she muttered, her voice climbing with impatience.

"Livingstone."

With a hard breath she murmured, "Someone doesn't want your kind in the limelight anymore."

I flinched at her words, thinking of all the strange occurrences of late, the sick Vamps. Her words resonated with everything. "Who are you? How do you know this?"

"Morghanna." Nero's Mom stepped out of the entrance. She cast a panicked glance toward me, and then the old woman. "Everything okay?"

"The Undead have come to dance again," the old woman snarled. "They will fall...it's inevitable."

Nero's Mom reached for my arm and pulled me. I stumbled, catching the momentum as she drove me toward the shadows of the stairs. "What are you doing here?" she hissed in my ear. "Where's Nero?"

I glanced over my shoulder to find the old woman was gone. Nowhere in sight.

"Mom?" he called from the top of the stairs.

She hurried him down with a wave, and the frantic thunder of his steps filled the space.

"This isn't a good time," she warned and cast a glance toward the shadows. "Things have gotten...troubling."

Fear crowded Nero's blue eyes. "What do you mean troubling?"

"You don't want to know," she murmured. "But you can't come here, not anymore. Stay away, call me if there's trouble. But don't come near us, *you understand me, Nero?*"

The way she said it made my skin crawl.

She lifted her gaze. "The Witches are angry."

"It's to do with the diamonds, isn't it?" I reached into my pocket and grasped the bag.

Her gaze followed the movement, catching on the

purple bag. Confusion filled her, her brow furrowed, her breath caught.

She shook her head, her eyes widening as I dragged the purple bag from my pocket.

"Show me," her voice was guttural and strange.

She hadn't wanted to see them before. But now...now there was fear.

I reached in, grasped a few of them and pulled them out. The diamonds were broken inside, but they were still intact, one half of the jewel was black, and the other clear.

"One side fighting with the other," she muttered, her voice crackling with fear as she lifted her head. "And the Vampire line grows weaker."

CHAPTER SEVENTEEN

SOMETHING IS IN THE AIR

And the Vampire line grows weaker.

I tried to curl my feet under my body, closing in, pulling away.

"Hey," Nero reached out and touched my arm. "You okay?"

I tried to nod, but it just wasn't in me. I was sick... all Vamps were sick. I watched the overhead lights blur as we passed them. One after another, they flicked out of view. Night swallowed everything else: the city, the cars, the skyscrapers.

Might as well take me too. My muscles twitched, nerves frayed. I hurt. Heart hurt. Desperation hurt.

But that would mean quitting. *Livingstones are fighters,* Dad's words filled me.

I ground my jaw. I'd fight to the end; until there was no fight left in me.

I'd fight for my family.

I'd fight for my line.

I shook my head, unsure how to feel. "Your mom said *don't come near us.*"

He never answered, just tightened his grip on the wheel.

"Us means Witches, right? She was telling us to stay away from Witches."

He just nodded and hit the gas pedal, pressing my spine into the seat.

"She didn't help us much," I added. Well, unless proclaiming doom and gloom counted.

Nero didn't respond right away, but kept driving, kept racing down the road. Only the rhythmic grunt of the motor kept us company. No other cars passed us, and part of me wanted to reach over to Nero and ask him to keep driving, to never stop, to make me somehow forget my life had turned into a massive knot and I had no clue how to untangle myself.

"She gave you those tea leaves."

I dropped my gaze to the console between us and stared at the sandwich bag filled with varied dried herbs and leaves.

They'll ease the pain, she murmured before pressing the bag into my hand and pushed me toward the entrance of the compound. *Go now,* were her parting words. *And don't come back.*

"I won't leave you," Nero murmured. "I'll help you figure this out."

Nero braked, pulling into the Academy driveway and headed for the main building. No lights were on inside, but the long driveway was lit with bright lights that haunted us as Nero drove the car into the parking lot.

A cold wind whipped around my legs as I climbed out and shut the door behind me and walked around the front of the car.

"Come here, take some of the Wolf warmth." He

wrapped an arm around my shoulder and walked with me toward my dorm.

But the cold stayed, slithering along my spine.

A shadow slipped between the trees, and then cut across the open in front of me.

It was the woman in black. The one from my dreams. My steps stuttered, drawing Nero's gaze.

"What is it?" He followed my gaze.

"Do you see her?"

Everything was silent. There was no wind. No sounds of animals. No sounds of anything.

The silvery moon lit up the woman. She stretched an arm out and opened her fist exposing a palm filled with black stones. She tipped her hand forward and the rocks tumbled from her palm. The moment they left her touch, they changed color from black to clear, glinting in the moonlight.

I touched the pouch in my pocket; my diamonds were still there.

She nodded as if sensing what I was doing, as if what she showed me was a symbolism. That in her touch, the stones were filled with darkness. What in the world did that mean?

"See who?" Nero stared around, but he seemed to look right past her.

I turned to him, my voice shaky. "Right there." I pointed but she was gone, and I stifled the urgent need to run for my life.

Nero hurried our walk, holding me so damn close we moved in unison.

Opening the door to my room, I pushed into the darkness, my gaze scanning for any intruders, especially on the balcony. That woman from my dreams kept haunting me.

This wasn't the first time I'd seen her around. Maybe I was hallucinating and going mad?

Nero remained in the doorway, the corridor light encasing him in a golden aura. He moved closer, his hand reaching out, cupping my cheek. I naturally stepped forward, desperation to not be alone wavering through me.

"I won't let anyone harm you."

"I know," I replied in a low voice, and the first burst of tingles swarmed down my arms.

He leaned in gently and kissed me, his lips warm and soft. I grasped his arms, holding on, drifting away on the wings of what he promised me—escape. He held my head with two hands and kissed me passionately, fiery, his tongue breaking the seam of my pressed lips. I opened myself for him, wanting him, needing him.

He broke away, and I gasped, burning up. A small whimper of anticipation fell from my mouth.

"Judas said to take care of you, and that's exactly what I'm going to do. First, I'm going to get us hot water and cups for the tea. So, get ready for bed."

He said *us*, not for me, meaning he intended to join me, and as much I bounced on my toes inside my boots, I held back my excitement. Something about not being alone flooded me with joy. Before I could respond, he turned and vanished down the hallway. I locked the door behind him and flicked on the bedside lamp, unable to stop thinking about his kiss. How delicious he tasted. How my lips still tingled from his. I rushed to get changed into my pjamas, pushing away the yawns that kept plaguing me.

I picked up the bag of diamonds from my desk and pulled open the ties. The once clear and sparkly stones now looked dull, darker. Why did they keep changing colors? Then I recalled the woman in black on the grounds earlier tonight, how they cleared once they left her touch. I could only assume this had to be the handy work of Witches. And was that woman the one who'd cast this spell? Except, she didn't look familiar to me. I tied the bag back up and left it on my desk, not wanting to deal with them now.

It wasn't long before Nero returned, carrying an electric kettle and two ceramic cups with the Academy crest and a strainer.

"Where'd you get those from?"

"I have my ways." Nero kicked the door shut behind him and busied himself to prepare our teas. "Your pjamas are cute." He glanced over his shoulder, eyeing my tee and silk shorts with zebras on them.

"They're misunderstood animals. I mean they're equids but are neither horses or donkeys, and they have the most gorgeous stripes. Did you know that the pattern on their coat is as unique as a person's fingerprint?"

"Didn't know that. Or that you're a zebra fan."

"Not many people do. Saw them once at a zoo with Dad and he told me no one knows why zebras have stripes, and something about that made me admire them. They have this secret no one knows about." I climbed into my bed and tucked my legs under the blanket, finding warmth, my eyelids growing heavy.

It wasn't long before Nero handed me a hot cup of tea, the herbal scent of aniseed and lemongrass flooding my scenes. "Your mom said these are safe for me to drink."

"People used to come to our home from miles to buy her teas, claiming they healed them." He eyed the spot next to me in the bed. "Can I join you?"

"Of course, I'm freezing," I answered without thinking, the desire to have him stay with me instinctual and needy. I drew back the blanket for him to get underneath for warmth.

He toed off his boots and got in next to me, the mattress bouncing until he found a comfortable spot. We sat with our backs to headboard, sipping our tea. The taste was subtle but it had a way of almost instantly calming me. Could be the whole placebo effect, or having Nero so close to me, but I didn't care. It felt incredible to feel something other than sickness and fear.

I slid my feet toward his under the blankets, and he claimed them between his legs as I said, "I don't mind if you stay the night."

He was drinking from his cup, his gaze widening from over the rim of his mug.

"I don't want to be alone, please."

Lowering his drink, he set it on the bedside table and turned to me. "Of course."

And with my tea finished and set aside, I flicked the bedside lamp off before sliding deeper into bed. With my back to Nero's chest, he collected me into his strong arms, and I snuggled against him.

His breath brushed through my hair. Despite the heaviness in my stomach from how terrible I'd been feeling over the past few weeks, my insides now fluttered at the feeling of his body pressed against mine.

"Want to know a secret," I murmured.

"What is it, beautiful?"

"This is my first time someone has shared my bed." The moment the words left my mouth, I regretted them. Stupid! What made me tell him that?

He kissed the top of my head, his breathing quickening. "Well, I'll be sure to hold you all night then."

"Deal." And I closed my eyes, not wanting to overthink anything, just enjoy the comfort he offered.

***

THE NEXT MORNING, I woke with a shudder, drowning in another nightmare but this time I was completely alone in a world that seemed devoid of people. Except, I didn't want to think about those nightmares because for the first time in too long I felt refreshed, my head was clear, and I was ready to jump out of bed and tackle anything. I rolled over to thank Nero for his company, for his mom's tea, but I found myself alone. A piece of paper lay on the empty pillow. I reached out and took it.

Morning beautiful. Loved being your first. Had to go to training. Didn't want to wake you.

I smirked to myself and pushed my legs out from under the covers, then plugged in the electric kettle to boil water. If the tea from Nero's mom indeed helped me, then I needed another cup. Then time for a shower, yet my mind couldn't stop thinking about Nero and how good it felt to sleep in his arms.

Swallowing the last gulp of tea, I dialed home on my cell. I'd been calling Dad once a week to see if he gained any insight on the diamonds. Three rings and Dad's croaky voice answered.

"Morwenna, is everything all right?"

"You sound dreadful."

He coughed, and I cringed because my dad never got sick. "Your mother and I haven't felt too well this past week. But you're sounding better."

I opened my mouth to tell him I'd visited Nero's mother, but I doubted he'd take the news of me going to a

Witch as good, and in particular when he grilled me about who Nero was. "I've been drinking a new tea with star anise and lemongrass. I'll give Chuck some to bring you." Part of me wondered if I ought to ask Nero to take me back to his mom's and beg her for a big batch for my whole family.

"Sounds wonderful, but I better go. I have a clan meeting in a few minutes. Love you."

"Love you too, Dad."

He hung up, and I turned toward the bag of tea leaves before opening it and sniffing. My skin didn't tingle with the presence of magic, or if it was, it was so subtle I barely felt it at all.

I stuffed the bag of tea leaves into my jacket pocket when Ava emerged from her room. She glanced over and smiled.

"Morning, babe. You're looking alive today." She walked closer. "Ready for breakfast?"

"For sure, I just need to do a quick stopover at Chuck's."

Her eyes lit up, doubling in size. "Let's go." She looped her arm around mine and dragged me outside.

On the third knock, the distinct sound of shuffling feet reached us from inside the hut. The door opened. Chuck stood there, shoulders curled forward, his face chalky, lips white, and eyes cloudy. He wore jeans and a hoodie, which was completely unlike him.

"What happened to you?" Ava blurted.

While I wouldn't have phrased it that way, I agreed. "What's going on?"

"Got a flu bug or something," he groaned, his voice croaky.

"Can Vamps even catch the cold?" she asked, staring at me for answers.

This was all about the diamonds. Not only had they

been affecting me, but it seemed it impacted Vamps outside the school too, like Dad. I dug into my pocket and pulled out the bag of tea, then handed it to Chuck.

"This tea mixture will help you, then please take the rest to Dad and Mom."

He sniffled and accepted the bag before retreating into his home, coughing.

We headed toward the cafeteria.

"Shit, he looks like hell," Ava added. "Maybe I should go back there and nurse him back to health?"

"Don't think that will work. Listen, you go to breakfast, I just have to go see Nefarious first. I'll catch up with you soon."

She eyed me, suspiciously. "You sure?"

"Absolutely. Will see you soon." We went in different direction, me following a worn path in the lawn toward the cottages where the teachers stayed. I just had to check the status on Mr. Leathers to confirm if this affected all Vampires or a select few. If he wasn't sick, then it might also indicate he could be involved in whatever was going on. After all, he'd appeared in my dreams and despite his insistence he was innocent, I needed to be sure.

On my fast walk, I pulled out the bag of diamonds from the inner pocket of my jacket and peered inside, noting the diamonds had turned a shade darker. Lately, they'd been changing, which just happened to coincide with Vampires getting sick. And I didn't believe in coincidences.

When I approached the teachers' cottage, Mr. Leathers emerged and closed the door behind him. Damn, he looked like death too, just as Chuck.

His gaze found me. "Morwenna, what are you doing here?"

I swallowed hard. "Came to check on you." And I

suddenly sounded creepy. "Chuck and my parents are sick, like me. So wanted to see if you were too. Seems all the Vamps have come down with something."

He ran a hand through his hair while pushing the strap of his bag over his shoulder. "Something isn't right," he croaked. "I'll be away for a couple of days with Vlad so I hope to have answers when I return. Until then, attend classes and stick to your schedule."

I nodded. "Of course."

And without pause, we both marched toward the main Academy building, towering over the land with its black pointy roof, and several levels of classrooms. It could easily be mistaken for a mini castle. Though most called it a mansion. Once we arrived, we went separate ways without a word and I headed to my first class of the day.

The next few days blurred into weeks and the time flew past.

Classes. Practice rituals and hunts, and more dance classes. Plus, lots of tea from Nero's mom to keep me going.

Later that afternoon as I headed back to my dorm, storm clouds gathered overhead and the first trickle of rain hit my nose. I hurried along the path in the darkened grounds. There were no other students around since most were at the cafeteria, but I didn't have the stomach for food.

Ava skipped dinner as she had a late class on shifter practices and would most likely attack the vending machines once she finished lessons.

I tucked my head low, pushing forward as an icy wind came rushing up behind me, leaving me covered in shivers.

The rains started.

Moving faster, I decided I'd ask Mom to take my winter coat out of storage if it was going to get this cold.

The gust of wind came again, more ferocious this time, pulling on my hair, my clothes.

"We will reign supreme once more," a deep voice growled in my ear.

I shuddered and spun on my heels.

Principal Stone emerged out of the darkness several feet away. Her steps slow and predatory. "You *will* be confined to the darkness, *blood sucker*."

I flinched at the sound of those words and shook my head. "Principal Stone?"

But this wasn't the Principal I knew.

This was a Master Demon.

Pale lips curled, revealing jagged edges of razored teeth.

Teeth that would carve right through me.

She kept coming, stalking slowly with seamless steps. I was hypnotized by the movement, her eyes glowed like burning coals. Black smoke fluttered from her body as if she were on fire.

"Ms. Stone," I mumbled as she lifted her hand and reached for my chest.

My heart.

She intended to pull the damn thing right out of my body.

And kill me.

My brain was numb and adrenaline thundered through me.

"Please, stop this."

Her lips curled against white teeth, her eyes completely black now, and stubs of horns pushed through her forehead.

With a sickening roar she lunged, crashing into me. Claws jabbed the middle my chest and pain followed. Digging. Piercing. Tearing at something.

A sharp pain jolted across my ribs. I whacked her hand

out of the way, recoiling, but her other hand moved too fast. Grabbing my neck, she squeezed, catching me off guard. With a fast kick, she knocked my legs out from under me.

I fell backwards.

The Demon was on top of me, her hand pushing against my chest.

I shoved my hands against her, kicking and bucking, but she was a mountain on top of me.

"The Demon's time has come," she snarled, drool seeping from the corner of her mouth. "We will *rule.*"

I thrashed and gripped her arm with two hands now, shaking in my attempt to push her back.

Fear came at me in waves. If my heart could beat, it'd explode. All I could think about was why the principal was attacking me. I flashed on her trying to destroy the diamonds weeks ago, her glares at me, the way she snapped at me at every chance she got. The only time she backed off was when Dad was around... If it wasn't for him, I suspected she would have kicked me out long ago.

She shoved down on my chest, and a gash of pain jolted across my chest.

In that moment of me screaming, fighting the demon, something new surged through me. It rose so fast that it tilted the world around me, just like the time I'd forced every shifter into a transformation at the same time.

This time instead of fear, I called to that dark power inside me, and opened myself to harness its strength. Catapulting down my arms, a surge of energy exploded from my fingertips, slamming into Principal Stone. She was flung backward, tumbling and rolling across the lawn.

I gasped for air even though I didn't need it, pure instinct had kicked in.

I scrambled to my feet, my whole body purring with power.

The rain fell hard now. No one else was around the grounds but me, and the principal who was trying to kill me. *Great.*

"Your death will show all Vamps, even your monster of a father that your kind are no longer in charge on Earth. Things are changing." The Demon unleashed a guttural growl so deep, it left me quaking. It shouldn't have, but what was rising from the ground wasn't the Ms. Stone I knew but something else completely. A Demon in its rawest form, disfigured, hunched over, claws and fangs, a body as dark as shadows, and only the pink of her tongue stood out as she licked her lips.

"You were supposed to take the diamonds to the Ancient and then come back, but you couldn't even do that. A complete waste of space, just like the disgusting Vamp from the sewers," she growled.

Her words thumped through me. "Y-you sent the Vampire to my room with the diamonds?"

"This is *not* what you're supposed to be." She pointed at my clenched hands, the energy sizzling over my flesh, prickling my skin. "Your power is cursed. Your power is abhorrent." Her noise wrinkled with disgust.

Was that how she saw me? As a courier to take the damn diamonds to the Ancient? Fuck! This was why she insisted I hold onto the diamonds after I accidentally forced the students in the school to transform into their supernatural forms.

"Why? Why Me?"

"Because you were the one who would lead us to him. You were meant to visit him, give him the diamonds. But instead you kept them, and they did something to you. But no matter. Now, I'll take the diamonds back. They don't belong to you."

With one shake of her arms, the claws on each finger merged and extended into swords, black as her soul, and I stumbled backward.

Oh, fuck.

Of all the times to not have the Wolves or Ava or Chuck around. They'd find me dead, my heart ripped out of my chest. Then Dad would turn psychotic and probably kill hundreds of souls until he felt he'd gained some form of revenge. And I didn't want my friends in that firing line.

Except, Principal Stone's admission rattled me. She planted the diamonds on me so I'd deliver them to the Ancient, then she probably killed the sewer dweller. But what was the big deal with the Ancient having the diamonds? I still remembered the sharp pain I'd felt when he touched the stones for the first time, his shuddering, the red eyes. That was why he pushed them back into my hands. They did something terrible to him--whatever Ms. Stone had intended.

In a flash, the Demon's agile movement had her darting toward me, swords raised, but instead of fear, a newfound anger thrummed through my veins.

The diamonds in my pocket trembled, and I felt them deep in my core.

I wouldn't die.

Not today.

I stood my ground.

Without hesitation, I tapped into the burning energy in my chest and let out a battle cry. I unleashed the energy rushing through, and it poured out of me as fast as a tornado. Tearing across the grounds in the form of a white fog, it collided into the demon, wrapping around her, strangling her.

She howled with agony, but for those moments, I felt nothing but anger. She'd tried to kill me. Take my life. Kill all Vampires. I clenched my fists, feeling as if I held onto the energy constricting the Demon. This wasn't my principal, but a monster, and I'd take her to my father and the Ancient and let them deal with her.

I moved closer. One step, then another, my fists curled tight, just like my insides. I had no clue what I was doing, but if I knocked her out, I could tie her up and call Dad. He'd know what to do. He always did.

But sudden laughter caught me by surprise, and I stopped just as a sword jabbed out toward me, straight for my chest.

Swiftly, I blocked the attack with the energy still humming inside me, driving it sideways, and I screamed as it poured out of me so fast it left me lightheaded. The power smacked into the Demon. It knocked her off her feet and sent her flying toward the woods. She slammed into a tree so hard all the branches shook. Birds flew from its canopy.

The Demon slid down and slumped into shrubs.

Frozen, I took in sharp, short breaths, shaking, unsure what I'd just done.

Fuck.

The faintest wisp of darkness emerged from the Demon's body, then dissolved on the wind.

I turned away, needing to run, but I couldn't move. Not until I made sure the Demon was indeed dealt with. What if it took down someone else? I'd never forgive myself, so I whirled around and hurried toward the forest, trampling foliage.

This was such a stupid decision. Stupid. Stupid.

Once I neared, I slowed, rain rolling down my face, under my clothes, soaking me to my bones.

I inched closer to the shrub the demon had fallen behind, my skin crawling. Behind me lay the school, but only the last threads of daylight remained. If I died my final death out here, no one would hear me scream.

But I pushed on and peered over the shrub, slowly. Needing to know.

Ms. Stone lay there in a tangle of limbs, unmoving, dead. No Demon form or sword hands, and now I was certain of what I'd seen rise from her body after her fall. Her Demonic essence vanquished.

Fuck. My hands trembled and my eyes teared up. What had I done? I turned and ran toward my dorm, through the pouring rain, through the puddles, though the fucking realization of what I'd done.

I'd killed Principal Stone.

CHAPTER EIGHTEEN

SIX FEET DOWN IS A LONG WAY TO FALL

I couldn't stop pacing from the door to the balcony, chewing my nails, convinced someone would burst into my room any minute now and accuse me of killing Principal Stone.

And it was true. I murdered my Principal.

I stifled the scream wedged in my chest. Not as if I meant to finish her, but she'd attacked me.

Fuck, fuck, fuck.

Killing any supernatural came with the punishment of death. The whole eye for an eye thing was popular with our kind. Dad would most likely get pulled into it too since I was considered young in Vampire years, and I'd heard tales of parents getting punished for their kids' behavior.

Hell! Sweat rolled down my back, drenching my skin. My fingers were curled into fists, and fear engulfed me completely. I felt trapped and dread was a knife in my gut, twisting.

When the familiar sound of a door shutting sounded, I darted into the hallway.

"Ava!" I hurried to her room and knocked nonstop until she opened it and stared at me with exhaustion.

"This better be life or death because I'm busting to pee."

"It is." I ushered her back into her room with a wave of my hand and kicked the door shut behind me. "Something happened. Something so fucking big." I gasped, unable to bring myself to say the words.

Ava took me by my arms and sat me on her bed. "Okay, whatever it is, we'll work it out. Just let me go bathroom before I pee my pants."

I wrapped my arms around myself, and rocked. But I couldn't wait a second longer and I blurted it out.

"Principal Stone is dead. Like you know, really gone, and I... I killed her. She attacked me, and I defended myself, but I don't even know why she attacked me."

"Wait...*what the fuck?*" Ava wailed from the bathroom. It didn't take her long before I heard the toilet flushing and she emerged, drying her hands on a towel.

I was shaking, then I lowered my hands to my side, unable to sit still. "Principal. Stone. Is. Dead."

"Like Dead, *dead?*" Her eyes widened.

I threw my hands in the air, stressed and filled with terror. "Yes, *dead, dead.*"

"Another one?" Ava half smiled as if unprepared to fully commit to a full joke yet. "Her body's not in your room like the last one, is it?" She laughed.

"Not funny, Ava. Are you even listening? I killed our principal."

"Okay, okay, slow down and tell me everything."

So, I detailed the whole incident, the Demon attack, my power, her Demon essence, and how I fought back like a goddamn superhero with powers.

"Holy fucking shit!" Ava tottered on the spot before flopping onto the bed next to me. It took her a while before she spoke again, and I swiveled on the bed to face her.

"They're going to punish me with death."

She was shaking her head. "No, they won't. You were defending yourself."

"It's my word against hers. No one saw us. And she's never hurt anyone else. Me, I forced everyone to turn into their animal forms."

Damn, was the room spinning? My mouth had dried and I could barely swallow. I was pacing again and I didn't remember getting up.

"Well, you saw the way she reacted to your diamonds in the gymnasium. We should have seen something strange with that. And hell, she's a Demon, and Dad always tells me I can't trust those soul suckers, no matter how much they integrate into our world."

I thought of all the Demons my dad dealt with, the boyfriend he'd tried to set me up with and who I insisted wasn't—Thorin—was also a demon. I didn't think they were all bad, but what if I'd been wrong, too secluded, too naive as Mr. Leathers had blurted out in front of Vlad? That'd mean I had reason to think the principal was up to no good...

"What I don't get is how this is all connected to the diamonds." Ava was on her feet and walked over to the windows before pulling aside the blinds to stare into the night. Rain pelted the window; I loved snuggling in bed on such days.

"I think our first problem is dealing with Ms. Stone's body."

Ava twisted her head to face me, already rolling her eyes. "I know what you're going to ask and it's no. I helped you hide one body already and that guy grabbed your boob and my neck muscles strained for a week from carrying the body into the basement."

"I can't leave her body out there. Someone will find her, and how long before someone finds out it was me? I used my power on her, so there's probably residue of my energy."

Ava sighed, her shoulders sagging. "Goddammit. I swear, you will owe me for life after this. And you have to promise me no more dead bodies. I mean, why can't you ever run in here and say you found a unicorn. That would be amazing."

That time I stared at her incredulously. "Really, unicorns? They don't exist."

"That's where you're wrong. Mom's cousin said he once saw one in Ireland."

I chuckled that time. "Was he with a Leprechaun?"

She nudged me with a hand but I dragged her into a hug.

"Thanks for helping me. This is freaking me out."

"Always got your back, you know that. Now, let's get this done before I change my mind."

We geared up in raincoats and boots, courtesy of my collection when the things were trendy. They might have cost me over five hundred dollars a pair, but they were washable. My Prada boots weren't.

Rain poured over my hood and rolled down my jacket. Ava and I hurried across the grounds in the night, each of us with a shovel we'd taken from the grounds keeper's shed, and a flashlight. We kept low and moved fast, water splashing under boots, the wind spraying us in the face. Even in the darkness, I saw Ava glaring my way.

"After this, you owe me a huge hot chocolate with marshmallows and whipped cream."

"Absolutely."

When we reached the shrubs near the edge of the forest, we stared down at Ms. Stone, and my stomach ached to know I'd done this.

"She's all muddy," Ava complained.

I reached down to feel her pulse against her neck just to be sure. Yep, dead. "Let's find a spot to bury her." Without a word, we drudged deeper into the woods, flashing the beam of light for the perfect place.

"What about there?" Ava pointed to an enormous tree, and I stared at her.

"A tree? You want us to bury her there?"

She shrugged. "Some customs put their dead in trees and all I know is that there's water seeping into these boots. How much did you pay for them again because they are useless."

"They're for looks. Anyway, maybe over there." I marched onward, my boots sinking in the mud, ignoring Ava's sighs.

"Here." I finally declared, staring at an open area, shrouded by trees. The grass had long ago died, so no one would suspect anything strange with the absence of grass.

I drove the shovel into the ground and thumped my foot onto the metal ledge to drive it deeper into the ground, then wrenched the handle back, bringing with it a pitiful amount of earth. "This is going to take forever!"

"We should go and get your three Wolf lovers. They'll have this pit dug in two seconds. They're probably used to digging up bones." She chuckled to herself before starting to dig too.

"Ha-ha. They're not dogs, you know. They're sweet, caring, and super sexy."

"They definitely are easy on the eyes, but they're too

much like candy for my liking. I prefer my men like whiskey."

"Have you ever tried the stuff? It's disgusting. Tried it once and I vomited for an hour." I drove the shovel back into the dirt and worked on our grave.

"You need to drink Poseidon's Whiskey. It's only available in my home town. Sure, could do with some now. Might warm me up."

"Maybe one day. But on the bright side, the rain's made the soil soft and easier to dig up."

Ava laughed forcefully and fake. "Nothing about this is easy. Not a single thing, and I change my mind. I don't want hot chocolate. After this, I want an hour-long shoulder massage. Oh, and my feet too."

"You're pushing it now." I shoveled more dirt out.

"Hell no, I'm not." We kept working, and I had no idea how much time had passed, but we now had a hole about four feet long and three feet deep. "Think we need to make it longer."

"Nope." Ava dug her shovel into the dirt and dusted her hands, the rain pouring down her face. "We're curling her in there and we do this fast. She's a demon who tried to kill you and is lucky she's even getting this grave. Plus, the rain's washing away our dirt to fill the hole and we don't have time to waste."

"Okay, fine." My muscles ached, so we tracked back to the body.

Once we got there, Ava gripped her waist. "You get the head." She hurried over to the feet, her boots making a sucking sound in the mud with each step. We heaved the Principal off the ground and waddled toward the grave. The rains were a blessing in disguise as they'd conceal our steps on the bumpy terrain.

"Is it bad that I don't feel as guilty as I should about her death? Think that makes me a serial killer."

"Ha-ha, if you're a serial killer for defending yourself, well what the hell are the real psychos out there? Babe, she was a monster and deserved what she got for messing with you."

"Thanks." I nudged her as we moved swiftly over the wet ground. Rain covered every inch of me and I no longer cared because I couldn't get wetter. But the worry still knotted deep in my gut that if we got caught, the Supernatural Council would demand my death. Not even my dad could save me. So, we were doing the right thing by hiding our tracks.

Once we reached the edge of the grave, we released Ms. Stone, and she slumped to the ground, splashing mud on us.

"Well let's get this done. I'm looking forward to my shoulder and foot massage." She smirked my way, stretching her arms in the air, all for show, when suddenly she was sliding, the ground under her feet slippery with rain.

Her eyes sprung wide, a panicked cry on her throat as she flapped her arms wildly.

I should have jumped to her rescue, but instead I burst out laughing as her smug grin vanished.

She slid into the grave, landing on her ass with a grunt.

I was tearing up from laughing so hard when a blob of mud hit me square in the stomach. "You didn't?" I stiffened, shocked at her assault, but couldn't stop sniggering.

She pushed herself to her feet, her pants covered in mud. "Give me a hand up." She stretched out her arm.

I stared at her with intensity. "If you pull me in there, your massage privileges are gone. Wiped from existence."

She glared. "You wouldn't dare?"

"Try me!" I stuck out my hand. We eyed each other like

warriors, but the moment she slapped her hand in mine, we both burst out laughing. I yanked her ass out of there and we stumbled on the spot.

The rain came down harder now, and without a word, we both rushed to the teacher's body. We rolled her in, her legs curling in front of her, and she slumped in there on her side.

"See, perfect fit." Ava reached for her shovel and starting hauling soil over the grave.

I hurried and joined her, covering Ms. Stone, trying not to look at her face. *She was going to kill me*, I kept repeating to myself.

When we finished, we tapped the grave with the backs of our shovels to squish down the Earth.

"Should we say something?" I said. "Final words, you know?"

Ava pursed her lips, her gaze drifting upward for a few moments. "Here lays Principal Stone. She was born, she turned into a bloodthirsty Demon, and it was over. She leaves behind students who are safer now, an opening for a proper headmaster, and a cactus pot plant in her office. Ding dong the witch is dead."

Ava smirked, proud of herself, and despite just burying someone, she had me smiling. With our shovels in hand, we turned away from the fresh grave and headed back toward the Academy. Just knowing I wasn't alone in this and had my best friend by my side made everything better.

CHAPTER NINETEEN

THERE IS NOT ENOUGH COFFEE IN THE WORLD FOR THIS SHIT

"How many of those have you had exactly?"

Coffee splashed the sides of the cup as her hand shook.

"I dunno." A nerve at the corner of her eye twitched when she spoke. "Five...six. You?"

I looked down at the ripples in my own cup, and all I could see was the cold, packed Earth of the grave, and Principal Stone rushing toward me with black, soulless eyes. I looked at my chest. I could almost feel her claws tearing at my skin. I shuddered and lifted my trembling hands. "I need another coffee."

"Tell me about it." Ava stared into nothing, dirt smeared over her cheek.

We'd come straight to the cafeteria after the burial, the rain washed us clean of mud, but we dripped all over the floor. They had warm blood here just as I liked it, and with the rain, the cafeteria was dead. Only the line of vending machines kept us company. I wished they placed the warm blood one in my dorm building.

"You weren't the one who fell in?"

I stilled, staring at my best friend before she slowly

turned her head toward me. The memory filled me, Ava with her hands flying everywhere, wailing as she toppled at the edge and slipped. "Anyone ever tell you, you have the reflexes of a bull?"

"Anyone ever tell you I eat Vampires like you?" She cocked an eyebrow and waited.

The corners of my lips twitched, and then curled, before I smiled. "My God, I never want to do that again."

"I never want *you* to do that again, either. You accumulate dead bodies like damn Wolves."

"Ava!" I lashed out, playfully slapping her arm, then lifted my gaze to the damn dance poster on the wall in front of me. "I want have a good time tonight. I just wish there was a way I could fix this goddamn sickness."

"I know," she reached across the table and rested her hand on my arm.

Sadness filled her eyes. I felt desperate.

Chuck was sick.

My parents were holed up inside, unable to attend any of their events.

Rumors were being spread about the end of Vampires.

There were many that would revel in my demise.

But Ava wasn't one of them.

I was weary and tired. I shoved from the table and rose. "I think I'm going to bed, and I'm going to stay there for a very long time. Maybe forever." I grabbed my empty cup and made for the stack of dirty ones on the counter. "Yeah, forever sounds good right about now."

Ava followed, plonking her cup on the counter next to mine before we headed out of the darkened cafeteria and back to our dorm. The rain had stopped, thank goodness.

We were almost there when I caught the scent of something sick and foul....and then something...very...*very*...dangerous.

I reached out, grasping Ava by the arm and shoved her behind me, murmuring, "Someone's here."

"It's me," Chuck's strained voice slipped through the night.

"And...*me*," the hoarse croak didn't sound familiar.

I stepped off the pathway and rounded the edge of the dorm, catching Chuck staring at Nefarious as he slumped against the wall of the building.

I took one look at both of them and winced.

"Oh, Chucky," Ava murmured and raced for him. "How are you now? Still got the vom's?"

"Don't talk about it." Chuck swayed on his feet and winced.

The towering Vampire looked beaten, dark circles under his eyes. His legs trembled, barely holding him upright.

Ava reached out and rose to the tops of her toes to place a hand against the warrior's forehead. "You're like an icicle."

"It's the sickness." Nefarious lifted dull eyes to me. If Chuck looked sick, then my teacher looked like he belonged in the ground.

He leaned against the side of the building, shaking and shivering. Whimpers slipped between his words.

"I thought you were..." I started.

"Dead? You thought I was d-dead?" Mr. Leathers stuttered.

"I thought you were gone," I answered.

He cast a careful gaze to Chuck. "I feel like I'm dead. The warrior found me waiting...."

"Sneaking more like it," Chuck snarled and bared his

teeth. As sick as he was, the warrior was ready to expend his last ounce of strength defending me.

"I came here to warn her." Nefarious cut Chuck a look of distaste.

"Warn me about what?" I took a step closer to the sickly Vampire.

"Someone is syphoning power off the Ancient. He's...he's sick, Morwenna. Very...*very* sick."

"Look at her, she's sick herself." Ava dragged a hand to her hip.

He did look at me, searching my eyes with his dull gaze. "But you're not, are you?" He murmured. "You're not sick like the rest of us. You're different. Something is preventing you from being like the rest of us."

"You saying I'm the one causing this?" Fear tore along my spine.

Nefarious stumbled forward and lifted a shaking hand. "No, I don't think you are. But you're still not sick, Morwenna. And you need to figure out why."

I shook my head. "It was the tea. Did you drink some, Chuck?"

"Yes." Yet he still looked terrible.

"Please," he whispered. "Can't you see what's happening here? The Ancient falls...and we all fall with him, including your family."

I flinched with Nefarious' words and wrenched my gaze to his. "That can't be." My stomach sank like a stone.

"Now you understand." He stumbled backwards, throwing out a hand to brace against the wall. "Figure out how you're connected, and then you'll find out how to stop this. You need to hurry, Morwenna. Before it's too late."

He shoved against the side of the building and stumbled away, leaving me staring after him. "I don't understand." I looked to Chuck who wobbled on his feet. "I don't understand any of this."

"You will," my warrior growled. "I'm prepared to stake my life on it, and Morwenna." He turned and curled his lip. "You need to come and get your pain in the ass rodent from my room."

Rodent? I tried to think... "Oh shit, the honey badger."

"Yes, oh shit," he muttered. "He's chewed right through my damn sofa."

I saw it now as he stumbled away. The back of his black leather boots had a hole in them the size of a golf ball. The pink skin of his heel peeked through the hole as he stumbled after Mr. Leathers.

"What now?" Ava looked to me.

Like everyone looked to me.

I swallowed hard and closed my eyes. "I wish I knew."

I'd killed and buried my Principal, and that was just the ending of a hell of a day. Right now, I just needed a hot shower, and to think. I reached out, grabbed my best friend's hand and we slowly made out way inside, and up the stairs.

The soft yellow light cast shadows into the corners of my room. I glanced around, stopping at the balcony and remembered all those nights ago where a scared creature stumbled in.

Did he know back then he was about to doom our kind forever?

"You okay?" Ava started and then stopped, shaking her head. "No, of course you're not okay. What a stupid question. What can I do?" She made for the bathroom and switched on the light.

But I still stared at the balcony, unable to think...unable to do a damn thing. The tap on my basin howled as water gushed from the faucet, before Ava ended the flow and strode out, wiping her hands on my good towel. "We need a damn plan." She came closer, and stumbled, catching her foot on the edge of the rug.

"Fuck!" She snarled. "That's the second time tonight."

The thick book from the Understudy class slipped from the edge of the bed and hit the floor with a *thud*.

"Sorry," Ava muttered and grasped the heavy thing from the floor. The cover was open, pages splayed for all to see. Something caught Ava's gaze. She wrestled with the damn thing, heaving it closer to peer at the entry. "Hey, does this look like the diamonds to you?"

She shoved the book toward me. I came closer, craning my neck to peer around at what she'd found. In the middle of the page were hand drawn diamonds, with the heading Dragon Tears above them. Ava lifted her head and looked at me. "Mor...this is it."

I shook my head. We couldn't get ahead of ourselves.

Couldn't get my hopes up...

"Says they're a vessel for power, that they consume and store energy." Her eyes widened as she lifted her gaze. It made sense...it all made sense. "And now you're sick...now your whole line is sick."

My mind buzzed with everything that happened recently.

"Ms. Stone said Demons are taking over from Vampires, right?" Ava murmured. "Maybe she was behind it all. Maybe it was just one crazy ass mutherfucking Principal."

"Maybe." I stared at the open book. "She wanted me to deliver the stones to the Ancient, to give them to him. So, if they're a vessel, what if they intended to drain the Ancient's power for themselves?"

Ava's eyes widened. "Weaken the most powerful, and the rest will fall."

I nodded, wrapping my arms around my middle. Principal Stone wanted to take down all Vampires. But why?

"Anyway, at least we have a starting point. You take this." She shoved the book at me. "I'm going to bed, and I swear to God if there are any more bodies I'm just going to give up."

I fumbled with the weight, taking the textbook before she turned away.

"Don't forget our outfits," she mumbled and made for the door. "And you better be ready for it. Because you owe me a goddamn party...your last one was shit. Not to mention my massage."

I chuckled as she yanked open the door and left.

I did owe her a party. I owed her a lot more than anything I could ever repay. I dropped the open book onto the bed and made for the bathroom, taking a shower, and then dressing in clean pjamas.

Were my diamonds the same as the ones in the book? I yanked open the pouch and poured them onto the open pages.

Black fought with clear crystal inside most of the jewels, but some of the diamonds were fully black. There were only a few that resembled the sparkling gems that were given to me. Nero's Mom had felt a dark energy then...feminine, and powerful.

I scooted down the bed and closed my eyes. The woman in the black shroud filled my mind. She'd held the black diamonds in her hand, before they fell. I could still see them sparkling midnight black before they glinted clear once more.

But then sleep claimed me...and I knew nothing once more.

"WHAT'S THIS?" I stared at the package wrapped awkwardly in *Happy Valentines' Day* paper. "It isn't Valentine's Day."

"I know." Nero shifted awkwardly. "It was the nicest paper I could find."

I glanced at the pile of massive boxes splayed across my bed, and then the tiny squished thing in my hand. The courier had delivered the dresses and shoes for the dance tonight, early as requested. When the soft knock came at my door, I'd assumed it was just one more mountain of stuff I didn't want to look at. Though I had to get ready for the dance now.

But this...this was a surprise.

"Well, you going to open it?" Nero murmured, his cheeks blushing red.

I fumbled with the paper at the end, tearing the wrapping. My fingers sunk into the soft black and white striped fur. I yanked the last bit free and stared at the plush zebra onesie. "Oh, wow."

I pulled it close and lowered my head to brush the softness against my cheek. "It's beautiful. I love it." I lifted my head and met his gaze. "It's perfect."

He beamed at the words, the smile brightening his blue eyes. "I knew you would. You said zebras were your favorite animal, and you've been cold, so I figured this'd keep you warm at night."

I did...I did say that, and he remembered.

My breath caught, desire flooding me like a bath of

liquid sunlight. I stepped forward, grasped the onesie in one hand as I threw my arms around him. "Thank you, it's the nicest thing anyone has ever given me."

He was so warm against me, so strong and healthy and I let myself relax in his arms, taking every second of perfection. His hold tightened, moulding my body around him, until his breaths were mine...his warmth was mine. He was mine.

"All we need is Judas, Bond and a little music, right?" he whispered in my ear. "And we could have our dance right here."

I pulled away then, looking up into his eyes.

Three heartbeats.

Three Wolves.

"That sounds perfect to me."

"But it's not gonna happen, is it furball?" Ava snarled from the doorway.

She shoved my door open and stumbled bleary-eyed into my room, looked at me from the corner of her eye and grunted.

Nero just chuckled and pulled away. "No, it isn't. Not until tonight anyway. See you then, Mor... I can't wait to see your dress."

"Are you getting dressed?" Ava asked after Nero left my room. "Dance starts in just over an hour."

CHAPTER TWENTY

YOUR ASS IS GIGANTIC IN THAT

I leaned closer to the mirror, finished the last touches on my mascara and eased backwards, staring at perfection. I didn't look sick under the pile of foundation and concealer. "Not bad.' I turned my head side to side. "Not bad at all." My skin no longer looked so pale, and my pouty lips were rosy.

My dark hair cascaded just over my shoulders, straight and shiny, pulled off my face with diamond clips. I twirled on the spot, my black evening dress billowing out around my legs, the heart-shaped corset portion of the dress hugged my chest, showing just the right amount of cleavage. Yep, the guys were going to adore me tonight. I twisted the diamond belt around my waist so the clasp sat at my back, and then I searched for my heels.

"You're not serious. You can't go like that?" Ava blurted from behind me.

I turned to find her in the bathroom doorway, taking up the entire space dressed in... "What are you wearing?"

She stared down at the pearl colored outfit that bulged around her, like some kind of beige banana.

Her head stuck out of the top and she wore black leggings and boots.

"It's my moon costume." She backed away and turned sideways, showing me the waning shape of the moon. Yep, there it was.

"That makes your ass look gigantic."

She shrugged. "Theme is black and white for a costume party. What are you meant to be? Persephone, Princess of the Underworld?"

"Hmm, I'm going as myself. I don't think this is a costume party, Ava."

She shook her head. "Nah. Black and White Ball means come dressed anything black or white, doesn't it?"

I headed out of the bathroom and she followed me to the balcony. Dance music already played on the wind and below were students headed to the dance, dressed in tuxedos and gowns.

Ava gasped.

I turned to her, took her hand, seeing her cheeks turn red. "I've got lots of dresses. You can borrow one of mine."

But her gaze was following the students outside, and she shook her head. "No. I'm gonna rock this as a moon." She twirled on her heels and marched back into my room, her moon tail wiggling with each step. "I don't follow others, and I want to do my own thing."

I adored her tenacity and individuality, but also knew the Cat gang would take this chance to tease her all night. I couldn't, wouldn't allow that.

"Give me two seconds to finish getting ready, then we're off."

She nodded, not staring at me, and it killed me to see my friend hurt.

I rushed into the bathroom, already pulling at the zipper of my dress.

When I finished looking amazing, I swung open the door and stepped into the room. "Let's rock this together."

Ava's head shot up and her mouth dropped open at seeing me.

"Do you like it?" I spun on the spot, dressed in my Zebra onesie.

Ava rushed toward me, her eyes glistening, and she threw herself at me, arms looped around her neck. "I fucking love it."

Her moon costume squished between us, bowling me backward and against the wall. We both giggled as she slipped out of my arms.

"When did you get this? And a zebra? Please don't tell me you're into Bronies. Or a Pegasister as they call females in this fetish. Don't ask how I know that." She giggled.

"I don't even know what you're talking about, but Nero got it for me today 'cause I adore zebras."

She lifted her chin and smirked. "We're gonna stand out tonight and everyone will want to hang with us."

"Yep, everyone sure will be staring at us. But for you, I'd do anything." I glanced into the bathroom, took one last look at my Gucci dress hanging over the sink, but instead of stepping into my glittery black stilettos, I headed to the closet and yanked on black boots. Facing my friend, I caught her swiping a hand under an eye. "You better not be crying."

She scoffed. "Right, as if."

Together we headed outside. Despite looking like a dork, I knew tonight was going to be special. And everything would be fine because I had my friend and Wolves by my side, no matter what.

"No one's ever done anything like this for me before." She sniffled.

I wrapped an arm around her shoulders and drew her against my side. "We're besties for life. And tonight, I just want to dance and pretend our lives are normal."

"You bet."

We walked toward the gymnasium. The music was so loud it left my skin tingling. Through the open doors, swaying spotlights lit up the place that resembled nothing of the gym we used for class.

"Nice costumes." A guy rushed past with his friends, chortling like pigs.

But I didn't care about them or anyone else. Tonight was about letting my hair down and not what others thought. Most of them disliked me, feared me, so what difference would it made if I wore a gown or onesie?

At the door we paused. The celebrations had started. People gyrated on a dancefloor that took up most of the room. Tables sat along the walls, filled with snacks and drinks. Black and white balloons dangled from the ceiling. Everyone was dressed up in the same theme, their hairstyles perfect, and me... I swallowed past the sudden realization of what I'd worn. My whole life, I'd been showered in only the latest brands, the most expensive; looking pristine was part of the Vampire look. So, going to a party in my onesie was new, but I was doing this for Ava.

The air tasted strangely of candy and a cocktail of perfumes. Everyone was staring at us, pointing, laughing. I didn't care.

"If you squint really hard," Ava started. "They all look like waddling penguins."

I looked around and locked eyes with Judas and his pack standing near the DJ. I grabbed Ava's arm and dragged her around the dancers and toward the Wolves who ignited the fire in my chest.

Nero and Bond stood on either side of him.

"Hey gorgeous." Judas reached out and took my hand in his. "You both look stunning."

Ava giggled next to me, while I was lost in his mocha eyes, adoring how he looked at me as if only I existed in his world.

All three wore black tuxes with small bows and looked so hot. They might be dressed in crisp, tailored suits, but each of them were so different, from Judas who stood tall, a glint in his eyes showing he was the leader, to Bond with sandy hair pushed off his strong face, looking deadly and delicious as always. The quiet ones always were. Then there was Nero, whose mischievous smile widened as he eyed my onesie, clearly loving what he saw.

The three of them leaned in closer, kissing me on the lips and cheeks.

I wanted to fall into their arms, have them surround me all night and lather me in their attention. Now this was kind of party I preferred.

Ava was tugging the sleeve of my zebra outfit. "Gah, do you have to do that in front of me?"

"If I knew this was a costume party, I would have come as my Wolf." A rumble rolled in Bond's chest, something about their animal side had me burning up. "Maybe it's not too late." He winked, and a giggle slipped past my lips. Damn, I was completely lost in their company.

"Drinks?" Nero asked, and we nodded. He and Bond were off to the drink table.

Judas hadn't released my hand, and his eyes were all over me. "I expect a lot of dances tonight, even in that hideous costume."

I pretended to look around. "Are you talking to me, the zebra?"

Ava huffed.

"Babe, I'll be chasing you all night."

"Geez, I knew I should have asked Chuck to come with me tonight."

I glanced over at her. "You can dance with us."

"Yeah, me, the fifth wheel. No thanks. I'm off to attack the snack bar."

Judas' hands fell to my waist and drew me against him, our bodies stuck together, his breath on my cheek. "You look gorgeous," he breathed. "Feels like we haven't spent enough time together, and I plan to fix that."

I stared up at the Wolf who captivated me. No one feature made him handsome. They all did, from the silvery hue in his chocolate eyes, to the squareness of his jaw, and then there was his bewitching smile. Whatever was happening between us was more than physical. He had the heart of a wolf, but the temperament of an angel. And when he looked at me, I felt protected and adored.

Nero and Bond returned, handing me a plastic cup with blood punch by the look of it. Bond searched for Ava, holding two cups.

"She'll be back." I scanned the room and found her in a hushed conversation with Salome not far from the doors.

My gut tightened, picturing her berating my friend, except, they were alone and they sure didn't look like enemies. More like friends sharing a secret.

I'd never seen them talking before, and considering the Cat bitches had tried to kill me, a spear of acid cut through me to see my best friend huddling so close with one. Salome patted Ava's moon tail and they both giggled.

What was so funny? I was the one dressed like a zebra!

"You're looking pretty jealous there," Bond whispered in my ear.

I waved him away. "Am not. Just worried she's picking on Ava."

"Yeah must be pretty harsh, with them both laughing," Nero added.

All four of us were staring their way, Judas at my back, his arms looped around my stomach. "Jealousy isn't pretty," he muttered. "Trust your friend."

I hated his words and frowned, but when Ava turned our way, we all acted like we hadn't been watching, and I suddenly felt stupid.

"Geez, can you guys be any more obvious?" Ava groaned.

I untangled myself from Judas' hands before handing him my cup.

"What was going on?" I looked toward Salome who headed back to Nesrin, both of them decked out in glorious gowns, hair curled and damn but they looked spectacular. But if I had my dress and stilettos, I'd outshine them in a heartbeat.

"Nothing. I'll tell you later." Ava reached for her drink from Bond, but I couldn't stop fidgeting with my pockets, feeling the diamonds because I didn't leave home without them. It just felt right to have them on me always.

I kept staring at Salome, laughing with Nesrin, and I collected Ava's arm and took her outside the gym.

"Didn't take you long," she teased. "I saw the way you were all staring at me when I was with Salome. She's actually not that bad."

"She tried to kill me, remember? Or are you just conveniently forgetting that?"

Ava flinched as though I'd slapped her. "I don't forget a thing, and *some things* aren't always what they seem."

I glanced toward the Lioness inside the party. "What were you talking about?"

Ava pursed her lips. "You're not going to wait until tomorrow, are you?"

I shook my head, my muscles tensing. "Just tell me."

"Okay fine. Brylee was the one who made Nesrin and Salome take your ring. Salome wanted you to know she didn't want to, but was forced to. She thinks you deserve to know the truth."

I swallowed hard, trying to process her words. "No one can be forced to do anything."

"They can if they want to remain part of a pride and not be isolated. They can if they have as much to lose as you do."

"I thought Nesrin was the pride leader?"

"I think Brylee fooled all of us. She's the mastermind behind that group. Anyway, look, no one's supposed to know. But Salome...she's okay. She's a friend even if it doesn't seem so."

Her words weren't making sense. "What—"

The sudden screech of a microphone had me flinching. "Welcome everyone to the Black and White Ball," Ms. Whitecotton's voice came from the gym. "Before we commence festivities and speeches, as is tradition, we shall begin with the Horn Dance. Everyone please line up and prepare."

I didn't move, wanting to understand why Brylee wanted me hurt. She didn't even know me.

Footsteps closed in behind me and I heard him breathing before he touched me.

"Let's go." Judas collected my arm, and I went with him, my head whirling with confusion.

"I want to speak to Brylee," I said.

Ava was alongside me. "Haven't seen her at the dance."

I nodded, though I couldn't get her words out of my mind.

Back in the gymnasium, everyone was arranged in two lines stretching the length of the room, guys on one side and girls on the other, just like in dance class.

Ava dragged me into line, while the Wolves stood across from us. And the music commenced. We were off, all of us, and there was something about having such a large number of people crammed together in a strange dance that had my adrenaline racing. I squeezed past Judas and Nero, both of them reaching for me. I adored their touches. On the way back, my phone beeped in my pocket, and I dug it out.

Just as I passed Judas, he frowned and snatched the phone from my hand, switched it off in a flash and stuffed it back into my pocket.

"No calls, babe. Just have fun tonight." His intense eyes had me listening to him, and I rushed forward as I'd fallen behind the line of girls.

He was right. I'd been so tense for weeks, sick, and uncertain. I deserved a night off. So I raised my head, smiled, and dove into the Horn Dance, letting the music consume me.

By the time we finished skipping in a large circle, the Wolves chasing us during the dance, everyone broke out laughing, gasping for air, and I couldn't remember the last time I laughed so much. Despite everything happening, a bit of time off was exactly what I needed.

"Let's get a drink." Ava seized my hand and pulled me to the tables, while I scanned the mass of students dressed up. Already Ms. Whitecotton was reaching for the microphone.

"Do you think it's too late to ask Chuck to join us?" Ava glanced at me with a smile in her eyes, then her mouth dropped and I followed her line of sight.

Brylee!

CHAPTER TWENTY-ONE

DEMONS AND DIAMONDS

"There she is, fucking bitch," Ava snarled. "I just wanna walk over there and smash her with my damn moon. Might get shit on it. Momma says if you hit shit, it splatters."

She was casting daggers toward the doorway. I lifted my gaze to see Brylee saunter in with a stunning floor-length sequined gown. Nesrin and Salome stood on either side, and for once the Panther was out-shone by the Cheetah.

The sting was instant as my nails drove into my palm. I wanted to know what her fucking deal was...why she urged the others to hurt me like that. "You have my back."

Ava squared her shoulders, smacking my ass with the corner of her moon as she turned. "Always."

I cut through the crowd, leaving the Wolves behind and stepped into her path. "Brylee."

"Vampire," she snarled, her eyes glinting.

I never even looked at the others. "Was it your idea to take my ring and leave me to burn in the church?"

She never answered, only cast a glance to her left. I followed her gaze to Ms. Lucas as Brylee muttered. "Where the fuck is Stone?"

"You gonna answer her?" Ava stepped closer.

Hate raged in the Cheetah's glare as she bared her teeth and snarled. "For me to know, and for you to squirm like the fucking worm you are."

"Right, that's it," Ava lunged.

I grabbed Ava's arm before she went all MMA Kracken smackdown on her ass. "Don't eat her."

My best friend just met my gaze and screwed up her face. "Eww…"

"Fucking eww me, Calamari Queen," Brylee spat.

My phone slipped from my pocket as I grappled with my best friend and hit the floor. "Great." Soft padding on my feet slid on the polished floor as I bent. I almost landed on my ass snatching my phone from the floor and then straightened.

But my phone was dead, switched off from Judas. I kept my gaze on the others, and took a step backwards. My fingers hit the button on my phone switching it back on.

The fight was barely over, tension still strained the air. But I risked a glance to screen.

Three missed calls from Mom.

My fingers trembled as I pressed the screen, re-dialing the call and watched them for an attack.

"Mom?" I jerked the phone from my ear and stared at the screen. But the line was still connected…and counting in seconds. "Mom, I can't hear you!"

"Mor-wenna." Her voice was a hoarse whisper. "I'm sorry…it's your dad. I think…I think he's…"

"He's what?" I murmured.

"Missing," she murmured.

Ava tugged my arm, dragging me away from Brylee and the other bitches. Judas strode toward me, his brow furrowed. *What is it?* He mouthed the words.

"It's my dad," I answered. "I don't understand what's happening."

The diamonds jingled in the pocket of my onesie as I moved.

"He went to see Tagar Lutherian," Mom cried into the phone. "But I haven't seen him or Thorin for days."

"What do you mean days?" I stumbled under her words, as the lights twinkled overhead and the slow dance music crammed my ears.

"Where Mom? Where did he go?"

But the phone was silent. The connection dead, the call ended. I yanked the phone away and stabbed the screen under the sheen of tears, punching the number for Mom and then listened.

"Come on," I pleaded as the number started ringing.

But there was no answer, only a voicemail. I ended the call and tried Dad's number. It was the same, the phone rang until the sound of his gruff snarl commanded me to *leave a message.*

"Mor," Nero murmured and reached out to touch my hand.

I'd forgotten he was there.

I'd forgotten they *all* were there.

I lifted my head as a tear slipped down my cheek. Judas was gone, leaving Nero, Bond, and Ava by my side.

A scream cut through the dancing crowd. Someone stumbled backwards as the diamonds in my pocket vibrated and grew warm.

"Now what?" Bond growled and turned toward the scream.

But Nero never moved, only lifted his gaze to mine. "What is it Mor?"

"It's my dad, he's disappeared." I shook my head, my whole body trembling.

"You said the name Tagar Lutherian, why?" Nero stepped closer and lowered his gaze.

Panic rushed through me at the sight of those blue eyes trained on me. "It's who Dad's gone to see."

Nero stiffened, and then swallowed hard. "Tagar isn't someone you want to mess with Mor. He's cruel, and he's the most powerful Warlock in the Blood Moon Coven."

"Blood Moon Coven?" I muttered. "The same one who runs the..."

"The Witches Academy, yeah." He cast a frantic gaze around us, searching for someone as another scream cut through the air.

"Why would my father see a Warlock?" I muttered.

"Demons!" Someone screamed.

"What the fuck," Bond snarled and took a step forward.

The Demon was a blur of darkness, rushing forward, and about twenty others swarmed behind him. Dark like invading shadows. I caught sight of Ms. Lucas, snarling and savaging, pushing her way through the crowd.

But she wasn't fighting against the others of her kind.

She was joining them.

I searched for Judas and fumbled for my phone, punching Chuck's number. "Come on...come on, Chuck."

"What is it?" The Vampire warrior snarled through the phone.

"Demons are attacking the ball," I snapped.

There was silence for a second, before. "I'm coming Morwenna. Take cover, defend yourself. I'm coming."

"Where is she?" Ms. Lucas snarled. "Where are the fucking diamonds?"

I swallowed hard, tearing my gaze back to the Demon

leader as one of the horde behind him lunged forward and savaged a kid. His screams had me shuddering. My breath caught as Thorin stepped out from behind a group of students and lifted his gaze to me. "No...no this can't be."

He was with Dad. Wasn't that what Mom said? He'd gone with Dad and....

It was the hallway attack all over again.

Only this time there weren't just two Demons.

There were at least twenty.

"Get behind me." Bond reached out, grasped my arm, and pushed. I stumbled sideway, using Bond as a shield as he snarled. "We're getting you out of here."

Nero scanned the students as the room erupted into chaos. One Demon was a blur, lunging through the air to savage the waiter. Ava screamed, stumbled, smacking into me with the top of her crescent moon outfit. I grabbed her, pulling her close against me. "Stay here, stay right here with me."

Blood spurted from someone to my left, splashing the floor as they fought and struggled. The coppery scent flooding my nostrils. The Demons were everywhere, swarming over us like a damn tsunami.

"Step aside, Wolf," Thorin growled. "Morwenna, you're coming with me."

I shook my head, staring into the blackest eyes I'd ever known as Ms. Lucas screamed out, "Demons will rule!"

My hand went to the pocket of my onesie, the diamonds clinked and rattled.

"I don't think so," Nero warned and moved to stand alongside Bond. "You'll have to go through us, Demon."

Thorin smirked, and it was the smile of a madman, or something foul and sickening and every bit the asshole I knew he'd always been. I grabbed Ava's hand as Demons attacked the students one after another.

Something flew through the air to hit Thorin in the face. Something soft and fluffy, and very...*very* violent. A Demonic bunny hissed and clawed, sinking blood covered fangs into the side of Thorin's neck.

The Demon howled, punched and beat the little thing, but the Wolves at my front weren't wasting a second. Bond turned, glanced at Nero, then room and snarled, *"move!"*

We ran, skirting the savagery as Demons lunged at the students one after another, sidestepping punches and throw-downs. Black eyes stared at me from everywhere as Demons swarmed along the sides of the room, closing off the entrances.

Bond slowed, and then pivoted.

They were everywhere, biting, killing, tearing shimmering black gowns and bloodying perfect tuxedos. Bodies littered the dance floor, torn arms jerking, and shuddering. Dead. Demonic bunnies joined the fray, lunging between attacks, biting Demons and tearing with razor sharp claws as we stumbled, turning to protect each other's backs.

"Stay together," Bond growled as a Demon stalked closer.

"The diamonds, *bitch*," the Demon sneered and lifted his hand. "Give us the power."

I swallowed hard and jerked my gaze to Thorin as he beat and tore into the ferocious rabbit at his neck.

The diamonds weren't just diamonds though, were they?

They were tears...Dragon tears.

A vessel for power. Power that seemed to be slipping from the Vampire line.

Behind the Demon the woman in the black shroud

slipped through the crowd, like they weren't there at all. *Or maybe she wasn't?*

I reached into my pocket and pulled out the purple bag.

A bag that had haunted me all these weeks.

A bag that seemed to obey one master...and it wasn't them.

"As soon as we heard you were coming here, we knew you were the one."

I jerked my gaze toward Brylee as she slipped out from the others, clearly working with the Demons. "And when you were made Understudy we knew it was fate."

"You?" Ava snarled at the Cheetah. "You really are a *spiteful* fucking bitch, aren't you? You wanted to ruin this..."

"I told you once before. *I'm a Cat!*" She glanced to the bodies and the screams. "You wanted '*a dance to remember*' wasn't that what you said?"

Ms. Lucas stepped closer. "We had a plan. Didn't take much convincing Principal Stone, or Thorin here, did it?"

"It didn't take much to convince me." Brylee smirked.

Thorin stumbled toward them, the side of this neck bloody and mangled. Still he swiped the back of his hand across his face and then turned to Brylee. She wrapped her arms around his neck, before kissing him...*hard.*

I almost gagged.

"You...you're in love with Thorin?" I muttered, unable to comprehend what I was seeing.

Brylee pulled away with a sneer on her face. "Thorin's been mine for the last four years. The only reason he put up with you and your *pathetic* family was because of this..." She threw out her hand, motioning to the horrific chaos.

The power, that dark *ravenous* power rippled along my spine once more. I took a step, meeting Thorin's gaze and shoved my hand into the bag of diamonds and pulled them free. "All for this?"

Brylee's gaze drifted to my palm and then narrowed, forehead creasing as she searched every obsidian filled stone. There were no clear sparkling stones now. They were consumed with darkness.

"They're not supposed to be black," she murmured.

Students screamed behind them.

Through the panic and the terror I found the woman surrounded by night.

"This isn't what you expected, is it?" I murmured, never taking my gaze from the corner of the room.

Nero's Mom's words filled my mind. *There's a presence...dark and powerful...and very feminine. But it's hiding itself from me.*

As I stared into the shadows of the room I knew the presence wasn't hiding herself from me.

"Nor is it something you can use," the words slipped from my lips. "It's something much darker, and *much* more powerful."

"*Fuck!*" Thorin roared, staring at the shards of darkness in my hand.

It was all for nothing. All the killing and the pain. My family filled my mind.

Mr. Leathers.

Chuck.

My parents.

The Ancient.

All for greed. All for power. All because of hate.

My throat choked at all the agony those close to me suffered.

"Take them." I lifted my hand as tears slipped down my cheeks.

"There's no stopping the inevitable!" Ms. Lucas snarled before she lunged.

But the darkness was consuming me, tearing through my nerves like wild fire.

The floor shuddered, and the walls trembled. Sparkling lights swayed overhead, casting the light across their faces as I lifted my hand.

The *boom* of power tore through my palm and out into the room.

I was the eye in this storm.

I was the commander and the cause.

I was everything. Every gasp of breath.

Every terrified scream.

Ms. Lucas stumbled backwards as Bond lunged. Pushed by the momentum, he slammed into the Demon teacher, knocking her off course.

They hit the ground with a brutal *thud.* Fists and claws slashed the air as Ms. Lucas tried to tear right through him.

Another came from the other side to barrel into Nero, tearing him away.

Leaving us vulnerable.

Leaving us to die.

As Brylee and Thorin came for us, I reached out to grab my best friend's hand. Ava was trembling, lifting her hand...her skin darkening to red markings as her eyes turned feral and strange.

I opened myself up to that darkness and swayed under the power. Those who were left in the ballroom fell to their knees once more.

"Mor,' Nero growled in front of me.

He was shuddering and shaking, lashing out to punch Thorin as he tried to hold onto to his mortal form. Somewhere in the room a Wolf's howl tore through the room.

The midnight diamonds in my grip burned. I opened my hand and lowered my other palm. Tiny fissures splintered the fragments, and the more power that filled me the more they cracked.

Ava let out a shriek and the unmerciful sound swept through the room. Cracks raced along the ceiling overhead. Debris and dust fell to the floor. I inhaled the power, the sound, and felt the diamonds in my hand turn to dust.

Dust that fell through the cracks of my fingers.

Dust that fell to the ground.

The sound from Ava ended. She stumbled, and then dropped to one knee, her crescent moon outfit cushioning her as she fell.

Movement came from the edge of the room, and I lifted my gaze to Chuck as he stumbled toward me.

He was alive.

He was alive and very...very drunk in his movement.

He scanned the room, finding me first and then Ava before he stumbled forward, stepping over bodies in his path.

One Demon reached for him, lashing out with wicked claws to grab his ankle as he strode by. But the Vampire was all warrior. He reached up, grasped a blade at his waist and plunged it into the Demon's chest.

The creature screamed and thrashed, but the fight was over in an instant. Chuck left only silence behind as the warrior came for us. He turned his head, took one look at Thorin and Brylee and curled his lips.

Thorin was ready, watching the warrior stride closer. "I don't want to fight you, Chuck."

The Vampire warrior just shook his head and moved the dagger from one hand to another. "That's because you'll lose, and if you think you're getting out of this alive, then you're as delusional as you are fucking ugly."

Ava shoved against the floor and rose to stand. Her body trembled as she took a step forward. "You're fucking ugly," she snarled. "I can see now why Mor preferred the Wolves."

Thorin growled, swung his dark eyes toward her and then rushed forward. Chuck moved fast, stepping in his path and with one savage jerk of his hand, drove the pure silver blade through his belly and then wrenched upwards.

Thorin paled, reached out, dark eyes finding not the Vampire who killed him.

But me.

"I...never...loved you," he murmured, and already black wisps floated from his body, as I'd seen happen to Ms. Stone.

I couldn't believe they were his last words, as though somehow he thought they would be my demise. Brylee stumbled backwards as her lover fell to the ground at Chuck's feet.

She turned, lunged, and sprinted away. Leaving the mess behind, like the coward she was. From the pack of survivors Nesrin stumbled forward. "Brylee!" she screamed. "Brylee get back here!"

But there was no coming back.

Not for her.

Not for any of us.

Bond shoved against the ground, and stumbled to his feet, but as weak as he was...he still turned to me. "You okay?"

I swallowed hard and nodded. "I think so." I took a step, stumbling forward to throw my arms around him. Nero neared, cautious at first. I didn't need to look into those blue eyes to see their fear and pain.

I hurt them.

And more than that...*I scared them.*

"What the Hell happened to you, hunky?" Ava stumbled toward Chuck.

He glanced around the room, surveying the damage, or maybe any threats, before he turned to the young Kraken. "Power...power like I've never felt before."

He turned toward me, careful, wary.

I lowered my gaze to remnants of midnight dust at my feet.

Power of the Vampires had now returned.

Returned to my line.

Returned to the Ancient.

Darkness filled the doorway to the dance hall as Mr. Leathers stumbled inside and looked around at the carnage, before he settled on me.

"Mom said you were powerful?" Nero's warm breath tickled my ear as he murmured.

I pulled away, staring into those deep blue eyes.

"You were powerful enough to stop this." He glanced to Ava and Chuck, and then Mr. Leathers and then searched the room. "Where the Hell is Judas?"

The phone buzzed in my pocket. I glanced down to find the caller ID...*Mom.*

As I hit the button and Mom's terrified words washed over me. "The Witches have him now, and I don't think they'll let him go."

The woman dressed in black only I saw held up her hand, palm extended toward me.

Carved into the center of her palm was a pentagram.

As I lowered the phone the woman in black turned to mist and floated away.

"Morwenna?" Mom's voice carried through the phone

as the last of the apparition swept away. *"Morwenna can you hear me? They have your father..."*

The woman in black wasn't any woman.

She was power.

She was darkness.

She was a Witch.

I turned to Ava and the others at my side. "We have to get him back. We have to save my dad."

The End

You're still here...well done. At this point we're not above bribery to keep you here....lol.
We hope you're enjoying Beautiful Beasts Academy and we hope you'll come and join the two of us in the Kila Foung Reader Group.
We'd love to share your favorite parts of the books so far and be part of our little crazy community.
We've got a lot planned for this series...and potentially another after this.
But you'll have to come and join us at Kila Foung Readers to find out more.
But for now, stay sassy...and a lot of assy.
Lots of love,
Kim Faulks and Mila Young.

HEXES AND HOUNDS

Love is complicated.

But then so is a stake through the heart.

There's a curse that runs through the Blackthorne Wolves.

Gnarled and Ancient. Unbreakable, they say.

It started with the Witches and now it's spread like a disease, infecting Wolves...

And now Vampires.

Livingstone Vampires.

Mom's frantic calls led me to the Blood Moon Academy, a dangerous place for any Immortal. I found dad there, chained like a beast, filled with rage.

And as everything changes around me, I'm sent a command from the Ancient...it's time to step up. Time to be the Vampire my kind needs to me be.

Understudy. Vampire. Daughter.

I don't know who I am anymore.

But I'll search for answers.

I'll do it all with the Wolves, my best friend and my bodyguard at my side.

And as the curse reaches out and marks my skin, I start to question everything.

How far will I go for love?

And, how far will love go for me?